The
REGRETS

ALSO BY AMY BONNAFFONS

The Wrong Heaven

The REGRETS

A NOVEL

Amy Bonnaffons

Little, Brown and Company
New York Boston London

Copyright © 2020 by Amy Bonnaffons

Little, Brown and Company
Hachette Book Group
1290 Avenue of the Americas, New York, NY 10104
littlebrown.com

First Edition: February 2020

Little, Brown and Company is a division of Hachette Book Group, Inc. The Little, Brown name and logo are trademarks of Hachette Book Group, Inc.

The Hachette Speakers Bureau provides a wide range of authors for speaking events. To find out more, go to hachettespeakersbureau.com or call (866) 376-6591.

Boots image on page 296 by Brittainy Lauback

ISBN 978-0-316-51616-7
LCCN 2019940324

10 9 8 7 6 5 4 3 2 1

LSC-C

Book design by Thomas Louie

Printed in the United States of America

For everyone stuck between this world and another;
for anyone who struggles to stay here

Mortal, your life will say,
As if tasting something delicious, as if in envy.
Your immortal life will say this, as it is leaving.
—Jane Hirshfield

I have scars on my hands from
touching certain people.
—J. D. Salinger

THOMAS

I remember what happened right after. I heard the first siren, and then the angel appeared above me: a gash of light resolving into the shape of a woman, with large feathered wings beating bright against the darkness.

The sight stunned me into silence, and I realized I'd been screaming. Now the world was still, and I was the center—pinned in place by the angel's gaze. She hovered above me for a moment, then descended to embrace me.

Now her soft chest was against my chest, her warm thighs wrapped around mine, the skin of her cheek against my own—if she could even be said to have skin; it felt more like concentrated light, warm and surfaceless. My body rose like a plant stretching sunward. The rough asphalt still pressed up against my raw back where my clothes had been torn away. I could still feel the gravel in my wounds, the pressure of a wrongly angled bone against the ground. I could still sense the presence of Therese's body, somewhere to my right, like a part of my own body that had been cut away. But as the angel held me, my pain drained like bathwater, replaced by something sweet and liquid—like honey, or melted gold. I heard myself moan with relief.

The angel brought her face within an inch of mine; we breathed each other's breath, like lovers. "Swallow this," she said. Then she placed a small black stone on my tongue. Simultaneously, she slid her other hand between my legs. I gasped, and my cock grew hard as bone.

I knew what was happening, and I was not afraid. I'd been waiting seventeen years for this exact moment.

But the next thing I knew, I was choking, and the black stone was flying out of my mouth, and my body was reeling away from the angel's as though she'd struck me: my skin shrunk back and my cock curled in, limp and useless. My body had rejected the gift.

The angel peeled herself off and hovered above me, her wings beating lightly. I could tell by the expression on her face—frightened, then clouded with doubt, then clearing in sudden recognition—that she knew what was happening. She folded her arms.

"We've met before," she said. "Haven't we."

The Officer sat across from me, behind a bulky desk made of cheap-looking wood—or more likely imitation wood, its grainy patterns suspiciously intricate, its surface giving off a dull matte half sheen. Behind him, two dusty venetian-blinded windows admitted no light at all. Twin phalanxes of green metal file cabinets bracketed the walls on either side of the desk. The walls themselves were made of a porous cream-colored cinder block, like petrified tofu. A brittle, curly-edged Civil War battle sites calendar was turned to MAY: APPOMATTOX. A yellowish-brown water stain, shaped like a cockroach, spread across the flaking plaster ceiling.

"So. Thomas Barrett," said the Officer. "Can you describe, in detail, what just happened?"

"I don't know," I said. "Can I ask a question first?"

He made a go-ahead gesture.

"Why do I feel like I'm in my elementary school principal's office?"

"I beg your pardon?"

"This room looks *exactly* like Mr. Antonucci's office. My elementary school principal. Not that I've thought about it much since my last visit there, but it's uncanny.

The color of the walls, the water stain. Even the Civil War calendar. He had one of those." I took in a breath. "Are you Mr. Antonucci?"

He shook his head tightly. "What is happening is that you are mentally enacting your conception of authority."

"Doing what? You mean I'm imagining this?"

"Your mental conceptions are shaping your visual perceptions. But I exist, just as strongly as you do."

He was not a large man; he wore a cheap suit, dandruff-flaked and tight at the shoulders. But none of this detracted from his dignity. His high bald brow was stately and imposing. He did look a bit like Mr. Antonucci, though not exactly: it was a loose translation. They could have been brothers. But the eyes were identical—dark brown, penetrating, hooded like an eagle's.

"So," I said. "You're larger than life. You've got impressive eyes and shoulders. But your furniture's so shitty."

"Excuse me?"

"I'm just observing. I mean, if this is my conception of authority, that's fascinating. It's like part of me respects you and part of me views you with contempt. Or despair."

"That's possible." He nodded. "But let's not get distracted by speculation."

"Sorry. What was your question again?"

"What do you remember," he asked, "of what just happened? Of what brought you here?"

Something about the combination of words he'd used—the word "remember" and the word "here," perhaps—set off a full-body tremor, or more like a full-body flinch. I found myself contracting, like one of those roly-poly insects that tightens into a ball when you graze its exoskeleton with your finger: folded up, with my head between my knees, breathing quickly and shallowly, protecting myself against what felt like an onrush of unwelcome light.

"Yes," said the Officer. "It's as I assumed."

"It's how?" I asked, managing—slowly—to unwind myself, to sit up straight again, to deepen my breathing.

"You're insufficiently dead," he said.

"I'm what?"

"Insufficiently dead. You lack rupture with your life. You have no exit narrative."

"Exit narrative?"

"Look," he said, standing up and pushing his chair under the desk; it made a rusty creaking noise as it scraped against the linoleum floor. "This is difficult to explain, but what you should know is that we take full responsibility. They're extremely rare, but these institutional errors do happen from time to time. I'm referring to April eighth, 1996, when you were nine years old. To what happened with Nineteen. It's a scenario we refer to as 'early exposure.'"

"Wait—her name is a number?"

"She will receive the appropriate discipline, of course.

You know, she got unlucky: if you'd been assigned a different Agent this time, you'd never have been able to identify her. That's what she was counting on. But it happened this way, so she confessed to the mistake— which is why you're here."

"So, then...what now?"

"Well," he sighed. "I believe that, in the end, you'll be glad for this opportunity. Most people don't get the chance to experience the state you're about to experience. In any event, it's highly educational."

"Wait a minute. Where's Therese?"

"Your friend? She had a narrative."

"What was her narrative? Where is she?"

"Don't get agitated, please."

I stood up. "Where is she?"

"Have a seat."

I sat down.

"I'm on your side, Thomas," he said. "I can't change the rules. All I can do is explain them to you."

"So, what are the rules?"

He slid a stapled document across the table, brittle and yellowed at the edges, in an antiquated font, as if it had been printed sometime in the mideighties and languished in a file cabinet ever since.

Please adhere to the following guidelines during the period of your re-manifestation. Everything about these guidelines, including their

stringency, has been carefully designed to pre-
vent regrets.

I looked up at the Officer. "What do you mean by regrets?" I asked.

"Regrets," he said in an announcer's formal tone of voice, as though reciting a definition. "Incursions of the past into the present. Threats to one's temporal integrity. An inability to coexist with oneself."

This hardly cleared things up, but I let it go. "What about Therese?"

He shook his head slowly, implying *No* to more than just the question I'd asked. With a throb of dread, I began to understand.

When I first awoke, after my visit to the Office—but no, "awoke" is the wrong word, because I hadn't been *asleep;* I had been somewhere else, or perhaps some*thing* else—in any case, when I suddenly found myself supine on the narrow twin bed in that small cold apartment, staring up at the cracked, stained ceiling, I didn't know, or remember, that I was dead. Nor that I'd ever been alive. I'd been wiped utterly clean. I was nothing and no one—a blinking cursor on a bright blank page.

For a period of time that could have been moments, or minutes, or hours, I existed like this, like a held breath. No, not exactly *held,* which implies a certain intention, a feeling of suspense. This was more like the space between breaths: at the crest of an inhale, right *before* it becomes an exhale. Precisely the space (I remember now, from the few sessions of meditation class I once attended) that the Buddhists point to as evidence of "nonself": what is the breath, can the breath be said to exist, when it is neither inhalation nor exhalation? By extension, can one's identity as a distinct and separable self be said to exist, in its similar state of perpetual change and becoming, never exactly one thing nor another?

I am trying to conjure this feeling in all its specificity because I feel a terrible nostalgia for it; I wish it would return. Because what eventually punctured this peaceful blankness was a sudden and massive surge of grief.

I still didn't remember what had happened; the feeling had no referent. I just knew that I had lost something, or everything—that I had *lost*. The grief rammed through me, tearing a jagged, ugly, guttural noise out of my body. Then I began to remember.

First I remembered the angel straddling me there on the asphalt. Then, piece by piece, other images began to return. I couldn't yet stitch them together—and yet on some bodily level I began to perceive the connection between them. The connection was me. I was a *me*, an *I*, a person.

Eventually, as this fact sunk in, my shudders began to subside. I found myself able to sit up straight, to take in my surroundings: a small room, perhaps eight feet by ten, furnished sparsely with a twin bed, a small metal desk and rickety folding chair, and a meager kitchenette (mini fridge, hot plate, sink). Through one door, partly opened, I glimpsed a bathroom; another door, now shut, presumably led to the outside world. The room's only other opening was a small window above the bed, its smudged glass guarded by vertical iron bars. On the small desk lay a crisp stack of twenty-dollar bills and a printed memo: ATTN: THOMAS BARRETT (REFERENCE #1037).

Something snapped into place, like a lock sliding

home: recognition, tinged with dread. *That's me,* said a voice in my head. *That's my name—Thomas Barrett.*

I had not chosen to come back. I'd been tugged back into this world against my will, by the thread of my own name: yanked from a cool blank nothingness into a web of cause and effect. Like it or not, my story was still happening; like it or not, I would have to write its ending.

You have been sent back to a place very close to the home you recently vacated, in a body that exactly resembles the one you left behind. Your return was necessary due to an institutional error, for which we sincerely apologize. These errors are rare, but they do occur. Errors include Mistaken Date of Death (error code 2578), in which the subject is delivered to the Processing Center too early or too late; Mistaken Identity (error code 1049), in which the wrong subject is delivered to the Center; and, much more rarely, Early Exposure (error code 3627), in which the subject encounters one of our Agents earlier in life and thus finds him- or herself unable, at the moment of final Consummation, to experience the potent mixture of shock, desire, terror, and awe necessary for catharsis and closure.

The period of your stay will be approximately three months. This window allows us to complete the procedures necessary to process your eventual arrival. When we are ready for you, you will receive a written communication from

14

us, detailing instructions for how to return to the Office.

The rest of this document outlines several important rules for the period of your re-manifestation. To be clear: we have no means of enforcing these rules, which exist for your benefit only. We can only warn you that, should you ignore them, you are almost certain to incur regrets.

The body you have been granted, while identical in most ways to the body you vacated, is nevertheless provisional and loosely structured. You may experience feelings of dissociation; numbness to sensation; excessive sensation; burning, freezing, or floating; and a loss of the ability to distinguish between mental, emotional, and physical realities.

For weeks after my return I could barely sleep, like a nervous hummingbird. I'd catch an hour or two and then snap awake, heart pounding, with the panicked feeling that I was in the wrong place. Then I'd look around the room, with its bare water-stained walls and Spartan dorm room furniture, and I'd remember where I was, and why.

By the time gray predawn light began to stream through the curtainless window, any further sleep was a lost cause. I'd get up, splash some water on my face, and go downstairs to sit on my stoop until the coffee shop opened.

This turned out to be my favorite time of day:

its coolness, its silence. The city looked scrubbed and expectant; the block crouched, hushed, like a tree just moments before all the birds launch themselves from its branches in one rustling swoop. In the morning my pain was mostly just the ache of being in the world, enfleshed and aware; I'd sit there on the stoop, opening and closing my eyes, gently trying to assimilate the unbelievable fact of this body.

You are responsible for daily reports of your activities during the period of your re-manifestation. These reports allow us to monitor your whereabouts. Mail your report at the same time each day, from the location specified on the attached map. In your report, break each day down into discrete increments of time and report on your activities during each increment.

At first I took the task seriously. I broke down the day into increments, as directed: *8:45 breakfast (everything bagel, scallion cream cheese). 9:00–10:00 read* New York Times *(Metropolitan, Week in Review). 10:00–11:00 rode bus to mailbox, mailed previous day's report.* But after a week or two of dispatching these missives into the void and wondering whether they'd even be read by anyone—or just deposited in some ancient file cabinet—the whole exercise started to depress me.

I decided to experiment with form. First I tested the waters with a simple slide into self-parody: *8:15 a.m. produced small fart; medium-sized fart followed 8:17.* Then I harnessed my attention to mental as well as physical

18

events: *10:07 p.m. experienced twinge of nostalgia. 10:08 investigated source of nostalgia, discovered Proustian memory link between buzz of apt. overhead light and similar buzz of empty fluorescent-lit college classrooms which would enter after dark to read in relative silence. 10:09 prodded by nostalgia, picked up book of poetry, read phrase "black milk of daybreak," realized how perfectly that phrase describes insomniac city sky—never entirely dark.*

Finally, unavoidably, I went meta: *Unsure how to break down increments of day. What constitutes increment? One hour? Fifteen minutes? A few seconds? Word "activities" seems misleading as well. Is not everything an activity, including the writing of this report? Should one include the writing of the report in the report? Or would such activity become self-defining, tautological, an Escher hand drawing itself?*

No matter how many versions I wrote, though, my reports all felt inaccurate. My thoughts and emotions seemed suspicious, of dubious origin. I experienced them in the third person. Here was a guy who looked like me, living some kind of life, interacting with things: the newspapers, the bagels, even the nostalgia. I didn't quite trust this guy. I overcompensated by paying extra-close attention, as if I could catch him in the act. Sometimes, I briefly inhabited the first person: for a jolt of surprise, or a brief saturation of pleasure. But then, inevitably, the past slammed up against the present, like somebody shouldering down a locked door: a rattle, a loosening, a rushing-in-of-darkness.

Structured activity is an excellent antidote to loose and dangerous thoughts. Enjoy the hobbies you practiced in your previous life—or try something new! Try to resist the temptation to tie your current "life" to your previous life. Remember: strictly speaking, you do not exist.

You do not exist. But I'd never felt my existence more sharply, the painful way you might feel the light in a room when it starts to flicker, when the bulb is just this side of burnout. Dozens of times a day, I started to fall out of myself and then snap, startled, back in. My existence buzzed and crackled. It was impossible to forget.

I tried to set up a routine. Each morning, I went to the coffee shop and sat there for several hours—mostly just looking around, observing the patrons as though they were zoo animals—marveling, as one does with zoo animals, at their exquisite self-absorption, their unstudied naturalness in their flimsy environment. I couldn't believe I used to be one of them.

This café was a place I'd strenuously avoided, in my previous life. It's called, simply, COFFEE, but the name isn't displayed anywhere, except on the menus. The storefront is mute, just brick and frosted-glass windows through which, if you bother to stop and look, you can glimpse the low wobbly tables, the paisley wallpaper, the gleaming futuristic hulk of the espresso machine. I'd always found the place pretentious, especially its name (so anorexically smug) and the coy withholding of it (what did they think they were, anyway: a twenties speakeasy? Did they find advertising too gauche? Did they fear the clamor of the unwashed masses demanding their walnut and Gruyère panini, *if only they knew?*). But it was only half a block away, and its ludicrous machine happened to make electrifyingly good espresso, and despite being dead, I blended right in.

I even came to feel affection for the baristas there, all hipster caricatures: the tall, leonine South Asian woman in baggy pants and suspenders over a tight midriff-baring shirt; the redheaded trans guy with the nose piercing and the T-shirts advertising bands I wasn't cool enough to know about (UGLY LITTLE DARLING, CHARLIE BROWN LOVES THE RADIO, VULVITUDE); the pale busty girl in the vintage dress and secretary glasses, a tattoo of a mermaid in a top hat spanning the length of her forearm.

I realized early on that this girl, mermaid tattoo, was actually someone I had met before. We'd once shared a joint at a roof party, sitting in a tight circle with a couple of other strangers. She kept calling me "Thomas Aquinas," for no particular reason—some kind of perverse anti-flirtation, or meta-flirtation. I'd volleyed capably, sure of the rules if not of what the game meant: her name was Meg or Maggie, but I called her Saint Margaret all night. We parted amiably; before I ducked out of the party, she grabbed my arm to hold me in place, then solemnly made the sign of the cross.

The first day I came in, I saw Saint Margaret at the helm of the espresso machine and froze. I nearly turned around and walked out. But the other barista, the trans guy, had already noticed me, was looking up in sullen expectation, waiting to take my order; I felt weirdly paralyzed, unable to break the social code and about-face.

As I stumbled through my order, my eye on Saint Margaret, I remembered the memo's words: You may be wondering how you'll possibly remain unnoticed, in the landscape of your former intimates and acquaintances. It may seem odd to you that we've provided you with no disguise.

Death itself is your disguise. No one is expecting to see you—so they won't. When Jesus appeared to Mary Magdalene, she thought he was a gardener.

When I left the café, usually around nine thirty, I'd catch the bus to the mailbox to mail the previous day's report. By the time I returned to my neighborhood, I was exhausted; I'd rest for an hour or two, then find some way or another to whittle away the remaining hours—walking, reading, attempting to paint—before I could officially declare the day "finished," and begin my description of it in the next report.

On one of my very first days I'd gone to the art supply store, gotten a canvas and brushes and palette paper and a few tubes of color. In the past, this—painting—was what had always worked most reliably to get me out of myself. It had nothing to do with "expressing" anything. It was pure displacement, the same objective I might have accomplished through tennis or gardening or the fussy concoction of a flawless ceviche, with lots of fresh-picked herbs and tiny knives. The drama of thwarted will, of attempted sublimation: eventually achieved, temporarily, like a pulse of open sky through the brain.

I'd dropped out of art school after one semester, when I'd realized that it was no different from business school: a backdrop for parties and starfucking, a generator of jargon. If that sounds snobby and self-righteous, well, I *am* a self-righteous snob about some things, but in this case I actually envied people like my classmates (Therese among them): their desire to share their work was fierce enough to withstand all the coarsening influences of the art world—the buffeting of the ego, the corrosion of exposure. I lacked that kind of faith. I feared that if my art ever made a name for me, that "name" would only smother me beneath the weight of myself; the whole point had always been disappearance.

I quit, and took a job managing the office of a small

design firm. I enjoyed the role. It fit me—and strategically obscured me—like a uniform. I painted and played music when I felt like it. And I assisted Therese when she started to take off as a photographer, to rack up clients and commissions.

This pleased me: she'd always been the real artist between the two of us anyway. When we set up shots together, it was she who had the terrifyingly precise instinct for the placement of an object or the angle of the lens; she who could anticipate, almost prophetically, the moment when the light would shift from cottony vagueness into spectral purity; she who understood the language of objects, their relational syntax, the web of meaning that could arise in the specific distance between a blue clay bowl and a saltshaker and be annihilated, or rendered cliché, if the saltshaker is moved half an inch too far to the left. After all our years together, she was exquisitely legible to me. In every furrow of her brow, every half-articulate direction, I read exactly what she intended, and executed it perfectly. I was happy to abdicate agency, to mute myself in service of whatever it was that moved with such authority through her. I felt like the manservant of a shaman, or the solemn, scurrying altar boy anxiously reading the gestures of an abstracted priest. After working with her I always went home and did my best painting; I was hollowed out and humming, I got to coast on the current we'd set in motion together, and at those times I had a feeling of wordless well-being that I can recognize, in retrospect, as gratitude.

But now, when I sat in front of the canvas in my tiny room, I experienced something like a panic attack: my heart started to pound, and I felt a thickening in my chest, and I had to put all of my effort into simply steadying my breathing. I tried to trick myself into painting; I covered the canvas in a light pink primer and then added a few slashes of blue, something deliberately abstract, and told myself, *See? You can do it.* What I meant was, you can paint something that has nothing to do with any of this; you can use this brush to take you out of yourself. But then one of the lines started to curve slightly so that it resembled her arched eyebrow, and I was gasping like a hooked fish, and I realized that no matter what I did, there was only one image in my head, Dopplering around like a siren, even in its departure always about to return.

Therese and I had been inseparable since childhood, when we'd lived in identical split-level ranch houses next door to each other in Oak Ridge, Tennessee, divided only by a low hedge. Both only children, we were drawn together by mutual structural loneliness, though our families couldn't have been more different. Mine were natives of the high-haired Cracker Barrel South, thrice-weekly attendees of the Church of Christ the Redeemer, owners of a house full of ceramic angels and throw pillows needlepointed with Bible verses.

They were also hopeless falling-down drunks. They managed to partially conceal this fact, thanks largely to the bright-faced denial of their church friends but mostly to my timely interventions. (I knew how to read the telltale weave in Andy's step, the slight increase in the shrillness of April's laughter; I grew expert at orchestrating excuses for us to leave public gatherings, including an alarming case of chronic Pretend Asthma. More than once I had to drive us home, my feet barely reaching the pedals.)

Therese's parents, on the other hand, were atheists and foreigners, scientists at the Oak Ridge labs; Adele was

Algerian by way of Paris, Tim a Jew from New Jersey. In New York they would have blended in perfectly, but in de facto segregated East Tennessee—well, Therese was the only even partially black kid in our entire school who did not come from the neighborhood that lay, literally, on the other side of the train tracks. I'm sure my parents would have objected to my association with the Golds— officially on account of their godlessness, not their race— except that I had no other friends.

Tim and Adele subscribed to *The New Yorker* and *Scientific American* and treated their daughter as a near intellectual equal, including her in their discussions of Modigliani or the oil crisis, regarding our play with distant amusement. Their house's interior was the opposite of ours: sparsely furnished, with a few uncomfortable thrift store chairs, some lazily framed modern art pieces, not a single doily or cut-glass Jesus figurine. Yet I always felt completely at ease there, able to relax, temporarily released from the strain of my eternal vigilance.

Tim let us borrow the expensive Leica he had toyed with in grad school; Adele took us to museums. It was in their house that I experienced other essential rites too: it was there I tried my first espresso, sampled unpasteurized cheese, and even, finally, lost my virginity, not without strenuous effort, high-fiving Therese against her headboard when it finally took, while Tim and Adele indifferently watched PBS downstairs. This was during the period, in high school, when we made a brief earnest stab at couplehood, encouraged by the fact that everyone already thought we were a couple anyway, undeterred by our baffling lack of desire for each other.

Once we'd achieved the trophy of virginity loss, we went our separate ways sexually; Therese went to Smith and discovered the personal and political advantages of pursuing pussy, while I entered a series of short-lived, fuse-blowing affairs with dark-haired women, mostly older (professors, bosses, aimless single moms who frequented the bars I tended). If Therese and I occasionally and half-heartedly pawed at each other when we found ourselves single and bored, I was mostly to blame for that. I was mostly to blame for most things.

When we were nine years old, when we'd been inseparable for nearly a year, Therese's family went away for
three weeks, to see Adele's relatives in Paris and Algiers.
Three weeks to a Tennessee kid during the summer—
especially a Tennessee kid with exactly one friend—is
an eternity: the yawning emptiness of the unstructured
hours; the sun sliding slowly down the day, like an egg
yolk on the inside of a glass; the ominous drone of
cicadas buzzing outside the window. Your blood grows
sluggish, your mind feels dead. It was on one of these
endless afternoons, while I read a comic book on the
floor of my bedroom, that the angel appeared.

There was no blast of trumpets, no grand entrance; I
simply noticed that a shadow had fallen over my book,
and then I looked up and saw her there. She was sitting
on my bed, serene and composed in her white draped
gown, her huge feathered wings spread out behind her,
spanning the width of the room. One of her wings lightly
grazed the tops of my Bible camp trophies, sending a
swirl of dust dancing into the air. She was blindingly
beautiful, bright against my faded red comforter and the
musty, muted yellow light of the bedroom.

"Come here, Billy, sweetheart," she said, holding out her arms. "Come here and sit on my lap."

My mouth fell open in protest—my name, of course, was not Billy—but nothing came out.

"Don't be afraid," she said, beckoning with both hands. "I just want to give you a hug."

I stood up and shyly approached her. Her long glowing arms closed around me, drew me onto her lap.

How do I describe the feeling of being held by an angel? Imagine the most transcendent, God-soaked music you've ever heard, then imagine yourself *inside* that music, imagine yourself *being* that music. Or think of the best orgasm you've ever had and imagine that it's taking place not just below your waist but in every cell of your body, all four chambers of your heart, even your eyelashes, even your fingernails. Imagine heroin, if it helps; I hear that's pretty great. Anyhow, imagine this: everything gone except pure pleasure, utter wholeness.

My body felt weightless, suffused with light. I was dimly aware that the feeling had edges—that somewhere beyond it lay my jagged nighttime terrors, my only-child solitude, the anxious responsibility I felt for my parents, for the world. But this new feeling begged the question: what *was* the world, anyway? The world began and ended in the cradle of this body. All the old darknesses seemed trivial—distant and silly, little pencil smudges at the edges of eternity.

"There, there, Billy," said the angel. She gently released

me, then reached back into the folds of her left wing and produced something. She held it out. "Take this and swallow it," she said. The object was a small black stone.

I no longer cared that my name wasn't Billy. I didn't care whether any of this was meant for me. When you've just been gifted the greatest pleasure of your life, you don't look it in the mouth. You don't consider whether or not you deserve it. You only want more.

I didn't hesitate. I took the stone, slipped it into my mouth, pushed it around with my tongue for a second—it tasted silty, like lake water, but also sweet—and then swallowed it. I felt it go down my esophagus, carving out a dark passage through my light-filled body. I was briefly seized by an uneasy premonitory twinge—but then the angel drew me to her breast again, and it instantly dissolved.

A few seconds passed. Then she leaned back, held me by the shoulders, frowned into my face. "Nothing's happening," she said.

I felt a dark, scribbly panic. "What's supposed to happen?" I asked.

She didn't respond. Instead, she frowned deeper and drew me in close again. But her embrace felt different now, anxious and clutchy. My panic churned and deepened. "What's wrong?" I asked, my voice muffled by her breast.

She held me again at arm's length, narrowed her eyes. "Open your mouth," she said.

I did. "Wider," she said. She inspected my mouth like a dentist, sliding her finger along the roof of my mouth and under my tongue. Then she leaned back.

"You're *sure* you swallowed the stone?" she asked.

I nodded.

She let go of me, looked distractedly out the window. "Well," she said. "Well, *fuck*."

I gasped. In our house, to say that word was tantamount to committing murder. In fact, I had never heard it spoken aloud by an adult. For the first time, it occurred to me to distrust what was happening.

The angel turned back to me. "You're not Billy," she said. "Are you?"

I shook my head, my eyes filling up with tears.

"Fuck, *fuck*." She clutched her lovely head, turning it from side to side. "Excuse my language. I have to go. I don't have a lot of time to fix this."

"Are you coming back?"

She didn't answer. "Be a good boy," she said. "Okay?" She mussed my hair distractedly, and then she was gone.

Just like that. One minute I was perched on her heavenly lap; the next, there was nothing beneath me but air. My balance thrown, I tumbled gracelessly off the bed and clunked onto the floor, slamming my elbow against the wooden bedpost as I fell.

"Ow," I said. In the now-empty room, my voice sounded small, a petty little-boy whine. I looked around. The room appeared exactly as it had before: the twin

32

bed with its faded comforter, the Teenage Mutant Ninja Turtle wallpaper, the dark blue shag rug, my *X-Men* comic splayed out to the page I'd just finished. Yet I could still feel the black stone churning around inside me, as final as the period at the end of a sentence. I got up, went to the bathroom, stood over the toilet, and tried to retch it up. Nothing came up but air.

I could still feel the dark passage the stone had traveled, my mouth and esophagus corroded by coal-colored emptiness. It was as if the stone had bored a hole through me, which I would always be aware of and would never be able to fill.

The next morning, when I came downstairs for breakfast, my mother was sitting at the kitchen table in her nightgown; in front of her sat a half-eaten bowl of cornflakes and a wineglass, drained but for the red dot at the bottom.

"Mom," I said.

She made a startled flinching motion, then said, "Tommy! Sweetie! You scared me."

"Sorry."

"Don't worry, precious." She smiled tightly. "Come here for a minute."

I did as I was told; I walked over to her side. She reached out and embraced me, drawing me in hard and fast, as if to snatch me out of the path of something or someone else. Of course, I couldn't help but compare this stiff, desperate hug with the lush embrace of the angel. My mother's skin smelled stale, her breath acidic.

I stood straight and slack-armed, enduring the embrace, actively trying not to squirm. Finally, she released me, leaning back while still holding me at the elbows so that my arms were pinned to my sides.

"Listen," she said. "Something very sad happened yesterday. Billy Phillips—you know Billy Phillips. That little boy, down the street, in the—" She gestured limply around her body.

"The wheelchair?"

"Yes." My mother hadn't forgotten the word; she simply considered it indecent to speak aloud of misfortune (or sex, for that matter) and angled whenever possible for others to do it for her. When it was necessary to speak these words, she did so in a whisper. "You know," she'd say, "he has *cancer*," or "she got *pregnant*." To this day, as far as I know, she still has never fully voiced a wide range of words, from "suicide" to "wig." (I experience a wave of pain and remorse now whenever I imagine her speaking—or not speaking—of my death. Its stain must have spread so evenly through her life by now that I wonder if any language has been left untouched; will she speak exclusively in a whisper for the rest of her life?)

She looked away, out the window. She seemed nervous to meet my gaze. I knew what was coming, but I didn't want to say it. "What happened, Ma?" I asked. "To Billy Phillips."

"He...well. You know how ill he has always been—

he has that *disease,* what's it called? With the *water* in the lungs, or on the *brain*—"

"But what *happened?*"

"Well, you know, there can sometimes be *complications* with things like that, you see, and—"

"He died," I said. "Didn't he." The word tasted sour in my mouth. My heart was pounding.

She closed her eyes. I could tell she was holding back tears. For all her flaws, April was an empathetic person. It was why she was so beloved at church, and also why—I often think—she drank so much: she couldn't stand pain, her own or anyone else's. She opened her eyes again and fixed them on me. "I just want you to know," she said, reaching out to clutch my hand, "how much I love you, sweetheart, and how much—"

I turned and ran, twisting out of her grip. I ran right outside, letting the screen door bang behind me, and leapt over the hedge into Therese's yard. I didn't stop running until I'd reached the cool silence of her tree house. There, I tried to cry, but nothing came.

I couldn't have felt guiltier if I had murdered Billy Phillips myself. Why hadn't I told the angel my real name? Why had I selfishly persisted, claiming an embrace that had clearly been meant for some other boy— that might, for all I knew, have saved his life?

Racked with the world-darkening guilt only a child can feel, certain that the black stone I'd swallowed was some kind of magic anti-mortality pill, I developed what Therese would later refer to as my Barely Disguised Death Wish. Not that I ever spilled my guts about the angel—that was the one secret I kept from even her. The single fault line in our friendship had always been her absolute refusal to countenance anything even remotely supernatural or religious. (Adele and Tim had once half-heartedly taken her to the Unitarian church, in an effort to keep up Oak Ridge appearances; it was Therese herself who called bullshit on the endeavor, with a tight, Gallic shake of the head, saying simply, "I don't see the point.") I couldn't risk her disbelief; she was all that I had.

I believed that I deserved to die. I also believed that I probably wouldn't, not easily, not in the way other people did, now that I'd been brushed by the angel's wing and swallowed her dark medicine. I began to test the waters. I leapt off higher tree limbs than I'd dared to before; I held my breath underwater till my lungs nearly burst; I rode my bike at reckless speeds, ignoring red lights, through the streets of Oak Ridge.

Nothing ever happened. Except that, more and more frequently, I thought of the angel, and began to feel other emotions mixed in with the longing and guilt. Was it really fair to punish a nine-year-old boy, a boy who'd spent his whole short life protecting his parents and averting disaster, for accepting a bit of pleasure and solace?

I even began to doubt my initial explanation—that I, in delaying the angel, had been responsible for Billy

Phillips's death. What if she had come not to *save* Billy but to *kill* him? What if that, death, was the purpose of the black stone—but it hadn't worked on me, because I hadn't been ready?

If so, perhaps I'd been nothing more than a brief snag in the angel's workday; perhaps our meeting—which had utterly changed me, in ways too deep for me to fully fathom—had been nothing but a mild inconvenience for her.

Over time, this explanation started to make more and more sense. I can't say why, except that sometimes, when a certain dark feeling arose within me, I thought I felt the black stone—or its echo, its ghost—pulsing within my body, and a sentence would resound in my head, as clearly as if I'd spoken it aloud: *I want to die.*

Yes, I decided, the angel had given me the black stone, the death medicine, but it hadn't worked—I'd been too strong, too young, too thoroughly alive. So she would come back someday, when I was in danger as Billy Phillips had been, when I finally hovered just this side of death.

So how far did I have to go? What did I have to do to see her again? How could I invite the chance to receive her embrace, to gain the release I desired? I imagined this hypothetical embrace as different from the one I'd enjoyed before: rougher somehow, more equal, a kind of struggle. I'd yell at her and she'd yell at me and then some kind of loosening would happen and it would all make sense. As I imagined this, I felt the stirrings of my first real erections.

One day, when I was eleven, I skateboarded directly into oncoming traffic and awoke trussed up in the hospital, with eighty stitches and seven broken bones. I hadn't intended to kill myself, not exactly. But I hadn't *not* intended to kill myself either. It was like an experiment in whether my will to live was stronger than this other will—to prod at the edges of life, to take the angel up on her game of hide-and-seek. Whether the humanness in me was stronger than this otherness also inside of me, this nonhumanness, whatever it was the black stone had given me.

I had faintly expected that the Will to Live would rise up in me, with Nietzschean glory, at the very last second—like a hidden superpower, the kind that animates an ordinary mom who can suddenly hoist a truck off her child trapped beneath. I thought that probably there was something inside me, some blind thrusting fist of über-vitality, that would surge up just in time to swat away the pale mothlike voice I'd lived with since the angel's visit, whispering the same brief fluttery phrase over and over into my ear: *What if?*

But nothing happened. I rolled my skateboard into the street, saw the car coming, calmly thought *I guess I'm really doing this,* and the next thing I knew, I was supine on a hospital bed, delivered into a totalizing bright-white pain—with no new answers, only a stronger sense of what my questions would cost me. The first sight that confronted me was my mother's pale face, mottled with tears. The first thing I felt was disappointment that she wasn't the angel.

During my recovery, I had a lot of time to think. For days I lay in my hospital bed and stared up at the swirling blades of the ceiling fan. Then I picked up a pencil (miraculously, my dominant left hand had escaped the accident uncompromised). Pictures poured out of me: angels, then devils, then disturbingly detailed dreamscapes, full of skulls and severed limbs spouting blood like fire hoses. I drew, from memory, a pair of lovely dark female eyes, and from those eyes sprouted maggots and worms and the charred skeletons of children. I overheard the whispered conversations in the hall: my parents' hissed accusations of the doctors, then of each other. Something was wrong with me that had not been wrong before. I was sullen and withdrawn. I barely spoke. I showed no interest in anything aside from my horrifying scribbles.

I was more than happy to accept the little pink antidepressants the doctor eventually prescribed. By the time I reached young adulthood, I'd ceased my search for the angel. Instead I looked for human women. They were easy to find. I'd been gifted with open boyish features, but I cultivated a hard look. I worked the lost-boy thing. Girls loved to look at my scar-mapped body, running their fingers down the raised white lines as if to erase them. I loved, and came to require, their looking. Unsurprisingly, I found I had a thing for brunettes. Most of the time I could ignore the white moth that continued to hover around my shoulders, whispering its two-word question. I ignored it most capably when I had a woman to plunge into.

Because of the *What if?* I developed a habit of standing too close to the edges of things, always. I liked the reactions I got when I perched on a balcony railing and calmly lit a cigarette. Some girl would clutch her face and say "You're making me nervous!" and I'd take a drag of my cigarette and say something casually philosophical about fear. Later the same night, kissing her, I'd murmur, "Thanks for getting me off the balcony," and she'd soften further into me, yielding up her deep center, and I'd feel so genuinely grateful that it was as if I'd been telling the truth all along.

Eventually, of course, gratitude would yield to selfishness, the illusion would yield to the real girl, her riddle would yield to the angel's, and that milky void would open up again; I'd ride across the Brooklyn Bridge at two in the morning, alone again, and think *What if?*

Those were the nights, usually, that I ended up at Therese's, drunk. Sometimes we passed out on her couch together watching some old movie; sometimes she had a date but let me in anyway, gave me a piece of cake and a stern talking-to before sending me home sobered up; sometimes I looked into her strikingly beautiful face, so familiar to me that I often forgot its beauty, and thought, *What is wrong with me? Why am I not in love with this woman?* If there's such a thing as an angel, a *practical* angel, then wasn't she all the angel I'd ever get?

Our last night was one of those nights. I'd driven my motorcycle—one of my dad's positive legacies; he'd bought the old thing and helped me fix it up—to her place, flopped down on her couch, opened my arms, and said, "Come here, baby, come to Mama."

In theory, *I* was comforting *her* that night—she'd just been dumped by a bi-curious surgery resident ("Fucking *straight* women, man. Will I never learn?"). I'd been in one of my dark moods all day, the moods that settled onto my body like medieval armor—a heavy helmet on the brain, a steel girdle constricting the gut. By the time I got to Therese's, I had to pretend a bright competence I didn't feel. I had to be the more intact of the two of us, at least temporarily. I'd brought a pint of ice cream and a bottle of bourbon, and we'd rigged up our favorite movie, *The Birdcage,* and settled ourselves on the lumpy couch, and I'd picked up her busted guitar and made up an impromptu song about the surgeon, Emily, and what a whiny bullshitter she was and how she might have been a brain specialist but Dr. Therese was a pussy specialist and her medicine was orgasms and now her office was open for business and there was no insurance she didn't accept…You get the picture. Therese laughed so hard she snorted, and then she said something about how Dr. Emily hadn't been that good in bed anyway, she'd been "afraid of my asshole." Then I got this very graphic image of Therese's ass, and redheaded Emily's nose deep in its crevice, and I couldn't help it, that woke my shit *up*—which meant, good news, that my body was coming out of its depression-armor funk, but, bad news, that I'd have to battle with it for the rest of the night, because Therese was nestling into me, head against my shoulder, soft cheek against my sleeve, and I could already feel myself unspooling.

As always, it was a kindness that did it in the end: Therese reaching up to wipe a dribble of ice cream off my chin. In my agitated state I mistook this tender maternal/fraternal gesture for a tender erotic gesture, and I leaned down, bringing my face close to hers, and our eyes snagged each other's, fierce gaze to fierce gaze, and she didn't pull away, and I leaned in to kiss her.

But before my lips could touch hers, she was shoving my chest away with her hand and laughing. She pulled back and folded her arms. "Dude," she said. "I'm pretty sure I'm gay. I'm pretty sure we were *just* talking about that."

"I know, I know," I said, briefly placing a hand over my mouth as if to remove the evidence. "I'm sorry. I just thought—"

"I honestly thought you were leaning in to pick

something out of my teeth. That's why I didn't turn away."

"Oh."

"Poor baby," she teased, patting the side of my face. "You're not getting laid tonight." She sighed. "Neither of us is."

"No, it's okay. The moment's passed, anyway." I laughed. "Sometimes I just see you from a certain angle, you know, the way other people see you, and I forget."

"Forget what?"

"That it doesn't work. When we try. Remember last time?"

We paused, remembering the last time we'd tried to hook up—about a year before—and shook our heads. That time, our strenuous attempts to maintain simultaneous arousal had increased to such a brutal pitch of futility that finally I'd flopped back down on her bed and sighed and said, "I feel like I'm at the fucking *Alamo*," and we'd both burst out laughing.

"It would be a lot easier if it *did* work," said Therese. She leaned back against the cushions and sighed. "If I were genuinely bisexual and you were—I don't know. If you didn't have your particular brand of damage. For which I feel partly responsible."

"How so?"

"I mean that sometimes I worry that I've stunted you. That you're like one of those baby monkeys in those experiments—you know, where they take away the mother monkey and replace it with a doll made of, like, wire and burlap. We've spent so much time together that your instincts about other women are all screwed up. I mean, both of ours, but *especially* yours."

"My damage isn't your fault, T. I promise."

She shrugged. "Well, what now, then? Want to finish the movie?"

"I kind of want to get out. Now I'm restless."

"Get out and do what?"

"I don't know. Go for a drive. Maybe go find some greasy food somewhere?"

"I know this Indian place that's open twenty-four hours."

"You're going to fart all night."

"I know, but who cares? No one will hear me."

"Right! That's the best part of being single. Farting with impunity."

So that's where we were going, on an errand of heartbroken sustenance. I didn't think—I *still* don't think—that I was too drunk to drive. I don't know what happened. All I know is that, briefly, I felt *okay,* deeply okay—roaring up the BQE, on a perfect midsummer night, with Therese behind me, her arms around my waist; this was the way our bodies best fit together, traveling comrades facing the same direction—buddies, partners as sexless as superheroes, a single interlocking unit, off on a mission. When we rounded that bend at Brooklyn Heights, the whole city skyline roared up into view and it gets me every time, that view: its arrogant vertical glory, its star-obliterating blaze.

Awe is dangerous. It is the last feeling I remember having before sky and earth traded places and we were flying in a *bad* way, and then it was all slam and scuff and scream and my last thought was *I have made a terrible mistake:* some error of attention, too much paid to the wrong thing.

Do not harass, molest, haunt, terrorize, seduce, influence, or befriend any individuals from your former life (this goes for their spouses and children as well). Do not seek out traces of your own past existence, or evidence of how you might have been mourned. Remember: that life no longer exists.

I managed to exert enough self-discipline to keep myself away from computers. Any day I could have walked into the public library, Googled myself, read my own obituary and Therese's, trawled social media for evidence of my friends and family—how their lives had continued, how they might or might not have publicly mourned my absence. There were faces I longed to see, facts I longed to know. But I feared this knowledge as much as I desired it. Plus, it seemed like a bad idea to intentionally disobey the Office's orders.

Yet I couldn't avoid seeing acquaintances. I ran into them all the time. This was the neighborhood I'd lived in for almost a decade. In the last five years, its trickle of gentrification had surged and crested. It now sported, in

47

addition to the fancy coffeehouse, a locavore restaurant, a loose-leaf tea boutique, and an artfully gritty bar serving IPAs and whiskey sours to the creatively tattooed. Even the West African place, after serving turbaned locals for years, had adjusted its message: GOAT HEAD STEW! read the placard outside. IMPRESS YOUR FRIENDS! My first day back, in a typically futile self-mocking/self-loathing move, I'd hit up the American Apparel on Atlantic: the tight-fitting jeans, the striped boatneck T-shirt, the faded blazer for when it got cool (I bought three of each so that I'd only have to do laundry once a week). I assumed that if I wore a uniform, I'd trick myself into feeling like a slightly different person, one I might take less seriously. I'd never been so grateful for fashion, its silliness and camouflage.

At COFFEE I often saw Jesse, a former NYU classmate, typing out his Ph.D. dissertation. In the time-honored manner of coffee shop strangers, he once asked me to watch his laptop while he went to poop; he showed zero sign of recognizing me, though we'd had many swinging-dick arguments over Foucault during college, and had once been goaded by our mutual friends into an arm-wrestling match at a dive bar (I'd won two out of three).

Another night, I saw my friend Todd stumbling out of the faux-gritty bar with his arm slung proprietarily around Apple, the ex-girlfriend of the drummer in his band, the band I'd occasionally subbed in on keyboards when their usual keyboardist got a better offer. Apple had often hung around after our shows and had tried several times, unsubtly, to sleep with me. Ironically, I was the only band member who'd never been attracted to her; I went for a certain type, and she was the opposite (loud, blond, openly wounded).

Had my death destabilized things so much? Had her shock at what had happened propelled her into Todd's welcoming, eczema-scabbed arms? I stopped on the street and watched them walk by. They didn't even notice me.

They'd probably already found a new substitute keyboardist too. A substitute for the substitute.

I'd never felt so fungible. Something swelled within me, a kind of panicked sadness that I didn't know how to expel, and I found myself following, walking briskly until I caught up as they paused at the corner to wait for the light. I leaned over and got Todd's attention. "Excuse me," I said. "Do you have a light?"

"Sorry, man," he said. "I just quit." He gave me a distracted, apologetic smile, then turned back to Apple. The light changed and they crossed the street, arms latched firmly around each other's waists.

Et tu, Todd? What kind of person *quits* smoking when his friend dies? Wasn't he supposed to still be immobile, perforated by grief? He looked so possessive and content, gazing into Apple's round upturned face. It was as if he had a whole new orchard of pleasures stretched out before him, nurtured by my decomposing body. "You're welcome, asshole," I whispered after him.

I knew this wasn't fair. But I realized now how alone I was.

Did it even make sense to use the word "I" anymore? I was like the photographic negative of a person, an absence given form, a loose ache of consciousness attached to a cheap facsimile of a body; I could blend in anywhere only because I belonged nowhere.

*You may experience intense resentment of people
around you. You may envy the way they are
unquestioningly lodged in their bodies. They
may appear anesthetized, half awake. Resist all
urges to "wake people up." Shocking them will
not have the effect you imagine it might. Plus,
you will incur regrets.*

Soon I shared, with Saint Margaret and co., the familiar, jokey banter of strangers woven together by routine.
S. M. herself turned out to be something of a genius.
One of those first days, I'd complimented her on the
intricate, perfect steamed-milk leaf she'd created atop
my espresso's tiny surface. "Is this actually as hard as it
looks?" I'd asked. "Did you have to, like, go to barista
school to learn it?"

She shrugged. "Took me a day or two to get it right."

"Do you always do the leaf? Or do you get creative
sometimes?"

"Oh, I *am* creative." She winked. "You think that's
a leaf?"

I knew the game we were playing here. I'd played it

often with girls like her, cool girls who shoehorned you into a sexual dynamic to prove they could control it. I squinted down into the espresso cup. "Oh," I said. *"Oh.* I see it now. I'm blushing."

"No you're not." She smiled. "But just wait. I'm very, very good at this."

After that, every day she made me custom espresso art that brilliantly walked the line between smut and cliché. Was it a snowflake or a snooch? A tree or cock and balls? A yin-yang or a titty fuck? Every day I loudly, vocally admired her artwork; I offered erudite, prurient exegeses. Sometimes the other baristas gathered round to see.

Yet I never learned a single fact about their lives. They never asked my name, or shared their own. If they thought it was odd that I showed up every morning at seven and stayed for an hour or two, mostly just staring off into space, they never let on. If all my theatrical interactions with Saint Margaret should somehow have made me more visible to her or to the rest of them—well, they didn't.

Most people don't notice most other people. Most people don't notice much of anything. Their lives fit them too snugly; noticing requires space. I suppose I'd always known this in an intellectual way, but now that I lacked a life of my own to envelop and absorb me—now that my life consisted mostly of strenuous attempts to impersonate a person—this seemed like the staggering central fact about humans.

* * *

At times, there was a fun side to my new anonymity: I
spent a few nights in bars, talking to strangers, making
up baroque lies, briefly enjoying the chance to be whoever I wanted—Suave Emergency Doctor Wes Bennett,
Shell-shocked War Reporter Jeremy Flank, Libidinous
Sculptor Ricardo Pierce.

But the game was too easy. Other people were so
embarrassingly credulous. "So you're, like, a *hero*," one
girl actually said, laying a fluttery manicured hand on
my thigh, after I'd told her about my stint with Doctors
Without Borders in Afghanistan, the time I'd tenderly
pulled shrapnel from a young girl's land mine wound,
looking into her dark quivering eyes and singing a low
lullaby to calm her, while her mother—who'd just been
gang-raped by warlords—huddled in the corner, weep-
ing and cursing George Bush.

The girl's name was Ashley or Ashton or something.
She looked as though she'd grown up riding ponies. Her
hair was the color of genetically modified corn. "I don't
like the word 'hero,'" I said, placing my hand over hers.
"You know who the real hero was? That girl was the
hero. Even now, every day she hobbles to school on her
crude prosthetic leg, determined to learn to read—"

"Don't they, like, punish them for that?"

"You have no idea. If the Taliban overheard her so much
as sing her ABCs, they'd cut out her clit with a scimitar."

She covered her mouth in horror. "They *do* that?"

I closed my eyes, as against an onslaught of unwelcome images, then took a sip of my beer. "You have no *idea*," I said, "what they will do."

Ashley/Ashton was *quivering* by now, looking at me with wet wide eyes, her body tense with reverence. I could see her nipples pushing up against the thin fabric of her shirt. I almost wanted to follow through—my contempt for her had reached a near-erotic intensity; I could almost feel the ghost of the imaginary mutilated Afghan girl hovering at my ear, whispering, *Do it, hate-fuck this girl with her intact pussy and her dumb hungry gaze, fill her up with the blunt savage cock of death—*

And that's when I knew it was probably time to go home.

I couldn't help but (self-reproachfully) feel that this new quality in myself was just an intensification of a quality I'd always had—this desperation sublimated into something Therese referred to as "male plague." I'd struggled against my own male plague: in my guilty reading of bell hooks and Judith Butler and all the queer theorists Therese foisted upon me, the way you might foist vegetable shakes upon someone with a junk food addiction; in my therapy sessions with Myrna. Knowing what I knew now, though, I couldn't help but (self-pityingly) blame the Office. I couldn't help but wonder who I might have been if April 8, 1996, had gone the way

it was supposed to have gone. I'd tried to explain it to Myrna, harder than I'd tried with the rest of my shrinks, those kind stern men and women who'd adjust my doses minutely, then adjust them right back, like an anxious writer inserting and removing a comma.

Oh, Myrna. Myrna, I miss you—with your slate-colored sweaters and your Susan Sontag gray streak and your lesbian partner and your two large, hardy dogs. That was all I knew about you—that was all the photographs in your office disclosed—but I could imagine the rest, the West Village apartment and the expensive olive oil and the handmade soaps in the bathroom and the earnest discussions, over late-night red wine, about whether or not to purchase a dilapidated country home or adopt a biracial child. Myrna, I'm making fun of you but I loved you. You refused to be charmed by me. When I teased you, you didn't tease back—you just looked at me sadly, as if you could see right through me, but couldn't quite name the thing that you saw.

Do not try to figure things out. Do not try to avenge anything, or to "set things right." We suggest that you simply try to enjoy this gift of time. Did you have a "bucket list"? Now is the time to knock those items off, for good! You won't get another chance.

Also: if you attempt to curtail this period through any form of auto-antagonism (read: suicide), you will incur regrets. Besides, it won't work.

I tried, I really did. I went to Coney Island one day and rode the Cyclone until I threw up. I walked all over Brooklyn and Queens, hovering in previously unknown-to-me ethnic enclaves for hours on end, sampling varieties of fried dough I hadn't known existed, getting into long conversations with rough-faced Ukrainian bartenders, playing chess with leather-jacketed con men in the park. I roamed the streets, sitting on random stoops, talking to whoever was around. I communed with a wider variety of people, with a wider variety of problems, than I ever had in my first life, my real life, because, well—I had nothing *else* to do.

In my first life, I had always remained snugly in the grip of my own relatively minor problems. Each night I went to bed thinking about tomorrow's office meeting, or the woman with whom I'd just been studying for the math test (this was my and Therese's euphemism for sex, our original unnecessary alibi to her parents), or the way that the latest adjustment to my antidepressants felt a little bit *off*. In the moments when I *had* encountered alien forms of suffering, I hadn't wanted to get closer— probably from some misguided fear of contagion. Now what was there to be afraid of? How could my own situation be any worse? I was *dead*.

But my communion with New York's lost souls showed me nothing new; it just deepened my awareness of the essential fuckedness of everything. I told one sad man or woman after another, in bars or on stoops or at bus stops, about how I'd killed my best friend—yes, killed her. I wasn't sure what had happened, but I was certain it had been my fault, an error deeply embedded in the flaws of my character: my self-absorption, my self-pity, my distractibility, my refusal to take life seriously.

When I spouted this monologue, my listeners just nodded, with unsettling looks of familiarity. Each of them had suffered through something just as terrible, or worse—though none of them had died doing it. In any case, none could offer redemption. They were all just sad and fucked, and trying to make the best of their fucked situations, and not doing a very good job. Knowing this didn't make me wiser or deeper or more Jesus-like. It just made me want to crumple into a ball. I wanted everything to go away, all of it.

So I started retreating again: drawing into myself, spending more time sitting at COFFEE, or reading on my narrow twin bed, trying to ward off the past and the present. Like a prisoner, I counted the days, marking them on a hand-drawn calendar on my bedroom wall—each day bringing me closer, I assumed, to that letter from the Office that would instruct me on how to return. I enjoyed the clichéd quality of this gesture, its narrative over-inscription, its thorough depletion.

I would have traded this sorry Lazarus half-life in a second for the chance to tell Therese what I'd never told her, to apologize and explain. Wouldn't she have believed my story anyway? Why had I doubted her? Hadn't her love been big enough to make room for some bright awkward angel? Or I would have welcomed pure oblivion, the nonexistence of this body that had caused me nothing but trouble. Again, more strongly than ever, I wanted to die.

And I could, I would—eventually. I had been back on Earth for almost six weeks, half the allotted time. In the meantime, I'd have to keep moving in my flickering half-assed way through the streets Therese and I had once walked.

There was nothing of her in any of these doorways, under any of these streetlamps. I didn't find her drinking in any of these bars or wandering any of these parks or sidewalks. Each time I saw a curly-haired, full-voiced woman, I lost her all over again. Each time I heard that crunch of bone, saw the bent limbs, heard that strangled cry that was the last noise her body would ever release— that body I had loved in my own sloppy yet ardent way, now reduced to street-dirtied carrion.

There's no way to assimilate a memory like that, no way to connect it to your current or past experience. At least, I thought, in this version of my life, nothing I do really matters. At least I won't be able to fuck anything up any further.

Was I ever wrong.

Should you be tempted to begin any new relation-
ships in this re-manifestation, please remember
that—contrary to appearances—you are, in fact,
dead. Your death is a terminal condition; while it
is technically incommunicable, certain symptoms
of it may be transferred to others. Sexual contact
with another person in this state is, perhaps,
the most efficient way to incur regrets.

To be alive even partially, I suppose, is to be betrayed again and again by your body—by its recklessness, its commitment to pleasure.

The body doesn't care what you've done, or what you deserve. It doesn't listen to warnings. Your body doesn't know you've just crashed and totaled everything that ever mattered to you, or that it, itself, is mostly dead. All it knows is that it has *some* life in it. That life, no matter how raw and fragile and doomed, will do what life does: reach out toward other life.

I first noticed the girl one August morning, at the coffee shop. She had dark hair and glasses and bright-red lipstick and alarmingly perfect posture. Unlike the regulars, who slouched over their laptops or sprawled proprietarily across the threadbare couches, this woman sat up charm school straight, looking lost in private thought, delivering tiny bites of cupcake into her small red mouth.

She seemed different from the other patrons, these bland sedated zoo animals: alert and uncomfortable, like a squirrel, or some other kind of nervous prey. Did she, too, intuit that everything surrounding her was treacherously provisional? Even when she got up—pushing her chair back beneath the table as if to correct the temporary displacement her presence had caused, placing her dish on the counter with deliberate precision—there was a tense, fraught quality to the way she doled out her attention. I wondered, with a wave of arousal, how this attention might bestow itself upon another person. For example, myself.

That day, I followed her out of the coffee shop at a discreet distance, and watched her walk to the bus stop, arrange herself on its low glassed-in bench. I hovered there on the sidewalk, unable to approach any further.

As I lay in bed that night, I pictured various parts of the girl, one by one. First, I thought only of her red lips. Then her pale slender throat. Then her cute butt. I couldn't manage the whole girl. I could *just* barely hold myself together against the feeling that I was about to come loose and undone. Already I was so overstimulated by everything all the time that just *living* made my entire body feel like a throbbing erect cock; the prospect of actual sex was terrifying and unthinkable. The slightest swoon of genuine lust sent my molecules racing, as if I was about to heat up into a liquid or gas.

I could hear Therese's admonishing voice in my head, the voice she'd always used when I confessed some new erotic obsession. *And how is this one different?* she'd ask, one eyebrow raised. *How are you going to avoid drive-by heartbreak this time?*

I'd mutter some bullshit about living in the moment, embracing uncertainty, being honest about my own limitations, and eventually she'd stop teasing, grow frustrated: *Thomas, I love you, but when are you going to grow up? You never move toward anything, only away. You just grab the nearest warm body and run for the exits.*

She was right—at least, she'd always been right in the past. And yet, and yet: what if this—the girl—was just what I needed?

Not a *relationship*, of course—I had no interest in dragging another person into the rickety haunted house of this half-life, in deliberately breaking the Office's rules. But just a little harmless crush, from afar? Just a little fantasy, a spike of pleasure to sustain me through the emptiest, most memory-haunted hours of my day—a reason, besides my appointed duties, to get myself out of bed each morning?

The next day she didn't come to COFFEE, but I took a chance on the idea that she might be at the bus stop again, around the same time. I had to catch my own bus there at some point anyway, to go mail my daily report; there was no harm in showing up a couple of hours earlier than usual. I told myself I wouldn't linger; I'd board my bus when it came, whether the girl was there or not.

I hoped only to sit next to her for a few minutes— that I might just be able to hold myself together against my awareness of her body next to mine, its contours and privacy and scent. This possibility alone seemed like reason enough for existing. It was its own argument against death.

In my defense: I barely existed.

The girl with the red lipstick, or the idea of the girl, was a bright vivid gash through my loneliness: the hideous loneliness of the dead, a loneliness I can only describe as both infinite and suffocating, like a loop of musty bandage, layer upon layer of it, tightening as it thickens, deadening as it pains.

In my defense: is there a form of love that's *not* a welcome unraveling?

RACHEL

I first noticed him at the bus stop one hot day in mid-August. He was hard not to notice. I'm not the kind of person to use the word "aura," but this man seemed to glow. Maybe it was a trick of his coloring: white-gold skin, golden-blond hair, green eyes that actually seemed to crackle electrically in certain lights. Even so, he looked distinctly sad, hunched forward on the bench with his elbows on his knees, staring off into space. Or perhaps into the dry cleaner's across the street—it was impossible to be certain.

When the bus came, I got on, but he remained sitting there. I continued watching him while the bus pulled away. He didn't move, but he seemed to somehow shimmer in place, rippling in the heat, like an optical illusion or mirage; by the time the bus rounded the corner I wondered if he'd been there at all.

But he was there again the next morning, and the next. He became a regular, always there when I arrived at the bus stop at eight forty-five. We took different buses. Usually mine came first, and I'd watch him as I left. In this way he came to seem like a permanent fixture of the bus stop, as though he lived there.

He dressed stylishly, in the same exact clothes every day: close-fitting jeans, striped boatneck T-shirt. He always carried a brown blazer with him, as though it might get cool, but I never saw him put it on.

There were many similarly stylish young men in my neighborhood. But these stylish men were never alone and almost never sad, at least in public. They'd saunter in and out of stylish restaurants, their stylish blade-thin girlfriends glinting beside them like swords at their hips. But this man always sat hunched and alone, looking both mournful and restless, his right knee bouncing up and down, staring out at the street with a last-chance look as if he'd be tested on it later.

I looked at him a lot. I touched him all over with the fingers of my eyes. Some men's handsomeness is a trick of the light and cannot survive such probing, but he held up. His handsomeness was not detachable from him. It moved when he moved. It had sinew and pulse.

Sometimes he looked at me too, but then looked right away, back at the street, as if he had no time to be distracted—as if he had more urgent things to do with his electric eyes. To which I thought, *Well, fine.*

I work at a library. Not a fancy university library, and not one of the large venerable city libraries with marble steps or grand lobbies or statues of lions guarding the door. My library is a squat, shabby brick building on a side street in a quiet outer borough neighborhood. Our main

68

patrons are elderly people who use the elderly computers to check their elderly AOL accounts, or who stop by to read the newspaper in Polish and then shuffle out with disgruntled looks on their faces, taking zero books. There are some toddlers during the day whose parents and nannies leave piles of sticky picture books on the Reading Together Carpet for us to clean up, and every day at around three, schoolchildren storm in and occupy the place for a few hours, loitering loudly, sitting at the large splintery wood tables to "do homework," which really means finding excuses to giggle and poke each other with fingers and pencils under their shirts, testing their newly pubescent bodies as if for doneness.

Technically, I am the reference librarian, but very few of our patrons require me for reference. I spend a lot of my time straightening things up and alphabetizing. I love alphabetizing. I live for the lulls when I can travel slowly around the shelves, straightening spines, re-ordering titles. There is something so soothing in this, some inner rocking that happens when I move through the books, not conscious of their content but just of their physicality, their presence in the world as containers of words organized into patterns. I touch them one by one, and one by one they are there.

Only two other people work at the library: Jo-Ann and Tanya. Neither of them seems to care much about books. Jo-Ann mostly creates these terrible after-school events where she dresses up like Ms. Frizzle from the Magic

School Bus and manipulates kids into making things out of construction paper. If you are a crazy person in New York there are many ways to shape your craziness so that its contours fit smoothly into the vessel of other people's expectations. For example, most kids believe Jo-Ann is the literal Ms. Frizzle from the Magic School Bus just because she has red hair and wears elaborate earrings. They believe that if they make construction paper bookmarks according to her instructions, she just might take them to outer space or inside the human body. They always leave with this half-disappointed, half-relieved air that says, *The world may be less magical than I'd thought.* Tanya is from Jamaica and a mom of three teenage boys; she has permanent dark circles under her eyes and a good yelling voice. She is a genius with computers and can fix anything. She is also a genius at keeping the kids quiet and making sure that homeless people don't leave needles in the restroom.

During lulls in my workday, I would sometimes close my eyes and think of the man from the bus stop, imagine what it might feel like for those electric eyes to linger on my face and body. I didn't picture him touching me, just looking at me. Would some chemical reaction occur on the surface of my skin and work its way in, communicate something silent and profound?

I hadn't had any kind of romantic relationship in almost a year. In New York, dating felt like public transportation during rush hour: brief spurts of headlong rushing energy, then long periods of waiting uncomfortably, bracing oneself against a series of casual violations.

The last guy I'd gone on an actual date with was a Buddhist. He'd just gotten back from Thailand, where he'd meditated in a cave, or perhaps on top of a mountain, one or the other, for a month. Not by himself, there were other people there, but they weren't allowed to talk. This seemed about right, that you couldn't get enlightened while talking to other people. But now he was talking. He kept using the phrase "penetrated by silence." I closed my eyes and imagined a bright, thrumming silence entering me like a penis, emitting these sort of white rays that muted my body's nervous noise. It seemed as though that was all I'd ever wanted. To be penetrated by silence. But when I opened my eyes nothing had changed: he was still sitting there, talking.

Supposedly, according to scientists, women are the more talkative ones—the verbal parts of their brains are all lit up, as opposed to the lit-up math parts in men's brains. I've found the opposite. The whole reason heterosexual men need women, besides heterosexual intercourse, is that they need someone to verbalize the world to. Or rather, in whose general direction to verbalize the world. It's like the way cats need a doorstep on which to deposit dead birds. Many women enjoy this role, or pretend to, but not me. There is a voice inside me, which I suppose is my voice but which I hear as if it's someone else's, the voice that says the words in my head when I read. My relationship to this voice is so intimate, so perfect, that most other people's voices feel like intrusions.

Which doesn't mean I don't get lonely.

The golden man's electric buzz grew stronger and stronger inside my head and body. Now he was touching me, and the touches felt like electric shocks, in a good way, like a zap that stunned my body into wakefulness. Perhaps he had been struck by lightning once, and survived with the lightning somehow trapped in his body; perhaps being touched by him would resemble being struck by small doses of lightning, dying and waking up, dying and waking up, over and over and over again.

I accepted the fact that the daydream had deserted him permanently. In truth it had gone almost as soon as we began seeing each other, but I held out hope that it would return. My hope lay in a kind of experiment, about sex. Mark was only the second person I had slept with, the first I had slept with repeatedly. I had a notion that the daydream lived in my body and that if he penetrated me in the proper way he could touch it, coax it out into the space between us, then step into it like a second skin. Mark was very game and strove to conjure every possible kind of orgasm, but in the end they were all the same. I mean they were typologically different but all daydreamless, purely physical in essence. I isolated the common denominator and concluded that my orgasms from Mark would never be different because they all came from him. When I cheated on him with my downstairs neighbor Kazim, to expand my data set, the results were mixed: the orgasms from Kazim were also daydreamless, but different enough to convince me that the daydream would probably return to me in a different form, with a different person, if it ever returned at all.

The unfortunate thing was that Mark never understood about the daydream. All he understood was that he had been betrayed and found wanting. I tried many times to explain, and he tried very hard to understand. Each time we failed, we both felt lonelier. The difference was that my loneliness eventually took on an odd beauty, like a pine tree on a bald mountain in an ink painting;

it made me want to actually be alone. His loneliness was suffocating, a form of panic; it made him want to get married. In the end I decided to study abroad in England and ignore all of his emails, and that did the trick eventually. He started dating his lab partner, and we never spoke to each other again.

Now my daydream about the electric man from the bus stop was growing in force; the daydream seemed to have attached to him thoroughly. Soon it would either draw us together or some crisis would occur that would cause it to evaporate. To delay the latter possibility, I avoided talking to him for as long as I could. I tried other methods of managing desire, of keeping it alive while preventing it from growing too strong.

For one thing, I told Flor about him. Flor is not my best friend, but she is my chief enabler. She is married to the only man she's ever slept with, the man she's been with since the first day of college, and she enjoys romanticizing my sex life. She actually uses that phrase, "sex life," as if I have multiple lives and one of them is just sex, sex, sex. "How's your sex life?" she'll ask me, leaning across the table and doing a little wiggle with her eyebrows. If there's something to tell, I will tell her, and then sometimes I'll say, "How's *your* sex life?," to which she always just shrugs and says, "I don't have a sex life—I'm married," even though I happen to know that she and Arthur have lots of sex: she is constantly getting

UTIs. So what she means by "sex life," I've concluded, is not actual sex but the aspects of it she has renounced: the danger, the randomness and stupidity, the excitement of an alien penis. I am skeptical of her nostalgia but receive a certain authorial pleasure from shaping my encounters with men into sleek narrative capsules for her enjoyment. She doesn't understand about the daydream, but I have discovered I can coax it into a sharper existence by enlisting her in my schemes for approaching the men to whom I hope it will attach.

"So you haven't even talked to him yet?" she asked.

We were having dinner near her office on Lexington, at our favorite Pakistani restaurant, a poorly lit hole-in-the-wall patronized exclusively by male taxi drivers and by us. We always sat at a corner table and talked frankly about gynecological matters while the men stared at Bollywood videos playing on a television mounted to the wall and pretended not to overhear us.

"Nope," I said. "I've only done the leg thing."

The leg thing is something I made up, which actually works. Try it sometime—you'll see. What you do is, when you feel a man's eyes on you, you uncross your legs and then recross them the other way. It is a simple trick but what it silently communicates is your sexual restlessness: it indicates the presence of an energy emanating from your general crotch area, which you can barely contain.

"Is it working?"

"Maybe, but he hasn't talked to me yet."

"Maybe he's shy."

"I don't know. He seems depressed, maybe."

"Hmm. Didn't you say you were going to stop dating depressed guys?"

"I said that?"

"Yeah. After that guy, what was his name...the weed dealer?"

"Oh. Drew. I just meant because he kept losing his erection. But I never knew for sure if that was from depression or from all the pot."

"Oh."

"This seems more like not the clinical kind, like he's just really moody. Like maybe he thinks a lot about existentialism or something."

"Oh. Okay." She scooped up some yellow potato mush with a piece of bread. "So what's your next move?"

But I was still thinking about depression. "Actually," I said, "'moody' is the wrong word. Because it's only one mood, and it's more like an attitude. It's like he's always on the verge of solving some sort of complicated problem that his whole life depends on, and like he can only solve it by sitting at the bus stop and concentrating really hard."

"On what?"

"I don't know. Maybe that's part of what interests me. Like, wouldn't it be nice to care that much about figuring something out? Wouldn't it be nice if something *mattered* like that?"

"Now *you* sound depressed."

"That's what Jimmy said." Jimmy was my actual best friend, whom I had not yet told about the electric man. "Jimmy told me that I'm depressed underneath the surface and I don't know it."

"Do you think he's right?"

I shrugged. "No. But if he's right, then I still wouldn't think so, so that doesn't prove anything."

"What's his evidence?"

"Well, you know how last year I went on that photography kick, then stopped? When I told him it was because paying so much attention to shapes was hurting my brain, he said that was a depressed person's logic."

She shrugged. "Jimmy's weird. I mean, he's great, but."

"I know."

"Anyway. Arthur's mom is depressed."

"Oh."

"She wants to divorce his stepdad, but she says she can't afford to. But she has this really expensive lizard. She could just sell it."

"What does Arthur think?"

"He doesn't have any room for his own thoughts. It's like he's his mom's therapist. She calls all the time. I mean *all the time*. And he can't say no. He has this suspicion that she prostituted herself to pay for his bar mitzvah and so it's like an unpayable debt." She pushed her tray away. "Anyway, I don't know why I brought this up. Look, I wanted to show you something." She flashed a wicked smile, her "sex life" smile, pulled out her phone, opened up the browser, and held the screen out for me to see.

It turned out she had just purchased his-and-hers butt plugs over the Internet for herself and Arthur. From her blush, her girlish excitement, I could tell that she had never tried a butt plug before. Somehow her excitement about the butt plug seemed connected to her frustration over Arthur's mom's lizard. They were two sides of the same coin, or something.

I didn't think about it too hard. I was busy acting excited for her benefit, which was easy because I actually did feel excited, for my own reasons. When I'd seen the butt plugs I'd been seized by an image: myself lying prone on the quilted surface of my bed, the golden man looming above me with a gleaming metal object in his hand.

The fantasy held power not because of any specific action the golden man might take next, but because of the feeling the scene contained: my total abjection before the daydream. Myself, limp-bodied yet taut with excitement. The daydream, erect and weaponized.

I barely heard anything Flor said after that. I had an idea for how to prolong the daydream without involving the golden man at all.

As I traveled around the library the next day, alphabetizing and straightening, I looked around to make sure no one was watching, and then I lingered in a section I had never explored before, one I had always disdained as the province of bored, gullible housewives. It contained titles like *Kama Sutra for Dummies* and *Unlocking Your Inner Goddess* and *Touching the Lotus*. I tripped my fingers along the spines and then pulled a book out at random.

It was called *Animal Breathing for Women*. I hid it under my desk all day and covertly checked it out before I went home. That evening I curled up with it in bed. *Envision yourself as an animal,* read the instructions for the first exercise. *If you don't intuitively know your spirit animal, consult a shaman or the Internet.*

One of the great misunderstandings of our culture is its insistence that sex should equal fun. In the animal world sex is usually not fun, at least for the female. With ducks, for example, all sex is rape. In order to come to terms with this truth we must come to terms with our animal self.

The way to imagine yourself as an animal is from the outside in. Begin with the skin. Do you have scales? Fur? Feathers? A salt-encrusted hide? Then take yourself slowly into your body. Go on a tour of your organs. Do you have the same organs as a person? At any rate, you have a heart. Take a moment and hear the beating of your heron heart or your sea lion heart or your chipmunk heart. At this point I stopped reading because the animal I had instinctively envisioned was a sea urchin, and I was pretty sure that they did not have any organs. I put the book aside and turned out the light.

Lying there with my eyes closed, I went back to my fantasy from the day before, of the golden man looming over me. It was still powerful; it still made me feel weak.

But now I had to admit that I could only generate so many fantasies before the actual skin of the actual man became necessary. In other words, there would be no way around this longing. Only through.

That Saturday—my day off, and an unusually mild day for this time of year: eighty and perfect—I went to the bus stop as usual, as if going to work, but I did not get on my usual bus. I just sat there and calmly watched it leave without me. From the corner of my eye I saw the golden man glance in my direction with a puzzled look; so he had been noticing me, was aware of my patterns. This gave me courage to execute the next part of my plan: when his bus arrived, I followed him on, swiped my MetroCard, and sat down next to him.

I had no plan other than to see what happened. At the very least I would learn where he got off. If the moment seemed right, I would make a bolder move, but usually I found that I didn't have to make bold moves when a man interested me. The bold move was just showing up. It's all about positioning. Men like to believe that they initiate things, but often they only initiate when the fruit is very low-hanging, when the fruit is right in front of their face, whispering "Pick me."

Now, sitting next to the electric man, I could feel a specific heat wafting off his body, as if he had a fever. This did not surprise or alarm me. It seemed consistent with my imaginings. He didn't look over at me but kept shifting in his seat, as if he couldn't get comfortable.

Finally, after the bus had gone a few stops, he turned and said, "You're making me nervous."

"Oh."

"Yes. It's something about your lipstick. It's so red. It's like a stop sign."

"Sorry," I said. "It's just my lipstick."

"It's okay. I just keep noticing it."

"What's your name?"

"Thomas."

"I'm Rachel."

"Rachel," he said. "Hmm. Not what I expected."

"What were you expecting?"

"I don't know. Nadia or Renee or something. Something more European-sounding."

"You think I look European?"

"Yeah. It's something about your haircut."

I reached up and touched my hair, as if I needed reminding of its shape. I've had the same haircut since I was a child, the same chin-length brown bob.

"So where are you going?" I asked.

"All the way to the end of the line."

"What's there?"

"I just have to do something. An errand. What about you?"

"Just running errands too. Nothing important."

Luckily, he didn't press me further, because I had not

come up with a specific excuse in advance. Instead, he started asking me lots of other questions about myself: what did I do for work, where did I grow up, what was my apartment like, where had I gone to college, what was my favorite vegetable, had I noticed the way a lot of girls right now cut their bangs in such an annoying style, way too short, as if an expansive forehead was a sexually desirable trait? (I had not cut my bangs that way—mine were long and off to the side, as bangs should be.)

I answered all his questions, and tried to get a few in edgewise about him, but he never let me. As soon as I'd answered he would either fire off another question or start talking, as if to himself, about my answer—he seemed to have many fully developed theories about me, most of them now confirmed. "Yeah, it makes total sense that you grew up in Maine—I knew you were a cold weather kind of person. I bet you can knit. Of course you like Almodóvar. Okay, who's your favorite Japanese writer? Let me guess. Mishima."

Before I knew it, we'd gotten to the end of the bus line. I hadn't intended to stay on this long, as it ruined my alibi—what was I doing way out here, other than following him?—but his incessant stream of questioning hadn't given me the chance to finesse an exit. Anyway, he didn't seem to care. It seemed that we were already past alibis. When the bus stopped, he nodded matter-of-factly, assuming I'd follow him: "This way. It'll only take a second."

I looked around. This was a desolate neighborhood I'd never been to, with weedy cracked sidewalks and wide streets strewn with broken glass and occasional storefronts proclaiming wares in Spanish or faded Cyrillic. Bare-chested men in gold chains guarded the stores against the empty streets.

We got off and crossed to the opposite corner, where a mailbox stood next to a bent streetlight. He took a sealed envelope out of his pocket, looked it over briefly, and put it in the mailbox. Then he turned to me. "Time to go back," he said. We sat down on a bench at the bus stop.

"That was it?" I said.

"That was it."

Silence. Perhaps his stream of questioning had exhausted him? As for me, I didn't know where we were, either literally or figuratively, but each moment I felt less and less certain that I wanted to be there. He was just as gorgeous as ever, but there was something unsettling about the way he talked. We hadn't really had a conversation so much as he had had a conversation, with himself, about me. Was I really participating yet, as more than a fact-checker? And why didn't he want to talk about himself? These questions pressed so hard on my brain that it didn't even occur to me to wonder who the letter was for, or why he had to mail it from this particular mailbox at the end of the bus line when there were perfectly good mailboxes in our neighborhood.

Just as I started to think it had been a mistake to follow him onto the bus, rather than leaving him safely relegated to the realm of my fantasies, he spoke. It was as though he'd been reading my mind.

"Sorry," he said. "I got a little overexcited before. It's just that I've been through a lot this year. Something really bad happened to me, and I've barely talked to anybody new since then, and it's like I forgot how to interact with people. And I don't know, I've just had this feeling about you. For a while. I like you." He paused, reconsidered his word choice. "I mean that I *register* you, very strongly."

"Me too," I said. "It's all right."

"I can't talk about the bad thing," he said.

"Okay."

"I'm not being coy," he continued. "I just can't. I also can't talk about the letter I just mailed. Also, I should tell you that I'm leaving in about a month."

"Leaving New York?"

"Well—yes."

"Why?"

"I can't explain it now," he said. "Sorry. That one requires a little warming-up-to. I just thought you should know."

I took this in. "So why don't you tell me something you *can* tell me?"

"Okay." He leaned forward, as I'd seen him do many times at the bus stop, elbows on knees, and thought for a minute. Then he sat up. "Okay," he said. "Here are the basics. I grew up in Tennessee. Two medium-shitty parents, no siblings. Came to New York for college. Went to art school, dropped out." He paused, as if unsure whether to continue, then plunged in again. "I have sloppy handwriting, but perfect oral hygiene. I've never had a cavity. I can play piano just well enough to fool some people into thinking I'm good." He glanced at me. "You still with me?"

"Yeah, I'm with you. By the way, I think that's our bus." It had pulled up to the curb and was idling, the bus driver leaning back in his seat and doing a crossword.

"Oh yeah." He stood up. "It won't leave for a few minutes, but we might as well get on."

We were the only people on the bus, and had our pick of the seats. We chose the two-seater furthest back. As soon as we sat down, our hands slid into each other's— casually, as if we'd been doing this for years.

"Are you hot?" I asked.

"What?"

"Your skin. It's so warm."

"Oh," he said. "That. Don't worry about it. It's just something weird about my body. I have, um…extra-fast circulation."

"Okay." This kind of made sense. "I actually have extra-slow circulation. When I give blood, it always takes me twice as long as everyone else. The nurses always feel bad and give me extra cookies at the end."

"How about that," he said. "We've got complementary weirdnesses."

"Complementary weirdnesses," I repeated. I liked the sound of it. This was exactly the problem I'd always had with the men I'd dated: either they weren't weird enough, or their weirdnesses were not complementary with mine. When you have noncomplementary weirdnesses, they just amplify and sharpen each other, collide at uncomfortable angles.

The driver put down his crossword, shut the sliding door, slowly pulled out into the street.

"Anyway," I said, "I have one question."

"Shoot."

"Have you ever been struck by lightning?"

"What?"

"It's my single theory about you. You got struck by lightning once, and you almost died, or maybe you technically died for a second. That's why your hair is golden, and why you're so...jumpy."

He looked pensive for a minute, as if the answer were complicated. "Something like that," he finally said.

I let it go. We talked about other things. I asked him about growing up in Christ-loving Tennessee: was it really as bad as they said? Did everyone own guns? Did he have to go to Jesus camp? These notions were thoroughly exotic to me; there were a handful of grizzled libertarians in my Maine hometown, but I'd never been to a red state before.

"Jesus camp," he said, shaking his head. "Did I ever. It's even cheesier than you'd think. I sang in the children's choir, then played piano for it. I wore suspenders and a gold bow tie. I can't believe it when I see the pictures now. I mean, it's so campy. Pun intended."

I laughed. "What else?"

"Well," he said. "Not to brag or anything, but every single year I won the Bible Verse Memorization Competition."

"Wow."

"It's not something I advertise. I mean, it's intimidating to some people, when they learn that about me. Like, they just don't see me for *me* anymore. All they see is the line of gleaming crucifix-shaped trophies..."

"They were shaped like crosses? Really?"

"I always used to think, I'm just so glad Jesus wasn't guillotined. Or electric-chaired."

"Or lethal-injected. Gold-plated syringes around all the nuns' necks."

"Yeah. But you know? When you think about it, the cross was worse than any of those things. *Way* worse. Hanging up there for days, your broken bones just kind of dangling?"

I frowned; our banter seemed to have suddenly taken a dark turn. I wasn't sure how to reply. "Well," I said. "I guess there's no *good* way to die."

He closed his eyes and flinched.

"You okay?" I asked.

"Yeah." He opened them again. "Just a chill or something." But he released my hand, folded his arms, and looked out the window. I didn't understand why, but I'd lost him. He'd become tense and distracted. His eyes narrowed and his leg jiggled up and down.

I squirmed in the silence for a minute, then broke it. "Tell me one," I said.

He turned toward me. "One what?"

"A Bible verse."

He sat up straight, seemed to revive. He spoke in a clear, exaggeratedly officious voice: "'I saw a brilliance like amber, like fire, radiating from what appeared to be the waist upwards; and from what appeared to be the waist downwards, I saw what looked like fire, giving a brilliant light all round. The radiance of the encircling light was like the radiance of the bow in the clouds on rainy days.'"

I golf-clapped, wiped imaginary tears from the corners of my eyes. "That's beautiful."

"Thanks. It's Ezekiel."

"So, did you, like, *believe* it?"

"Believe what? Christianity?"

"Yeah."

"Mildly and unquestioningly till age nine. Fanatically from nine to eleven. Then not at all."

"What happened at nine? Jesus spoke to you?"

He shook his head. "Weirder than that."

"You can tell me," I said. "I've had some weird stuff happen to me too."

"Like what?"

"Dreams that predicted the future. But minor, stupid things. Like in elementary school, I'd dream someone was going to be absent from class, and then they would be. I could foretell outbreaks of chicken pox."

"This was weirder," he said firmly.

"Tell me."

He paused and looked out the window. The bus was slugging through Bensonhurst now, stopping at every single stop, picking up doughy old women laden with grocery bags, muttering in Spanish and Russian. He turned back to me and raked his hand across his head, then dropped it back into his lap. His golden hair stood up in spikes. "Actually," he said, "it's really hard to explain. Maybe now's not the best time."

"That's okay," I said.

I reached over and took his hand in mine. This time, the touch was even more charged than before; it pulsed through me, lighting up my bones like an X-ray. The feeling must have been mutual: we looked at each other, blinking and wide-eyed, surprise rippling between us like heat.

We didn't talk for the rest of the ride. That was okay with me. I wouldn't have been able to pay much attention to words anyway. My focus had shifted to our bodies, to the way my hand fit into his, the way our clothes brushed against each other when either of us shifted in

91

our seats, the strong yet delicate line of his jaw, his clean and well-shaped mouth.

I grew more and more restless. I squirmed in my seat. I started to Morse-code messages into his hot palm. He probably thought it was foreplay, and it was, but I do actually know Morse code. I was a lonely child and I taught it to myself one slow summer out of boredom. Because of the particular book I used, I mostly learned anti-German war slogans.

By the time we disembarked at our stop, the one from which we'd begun our journey, so much had changed. U-boats lurked beneath calm Atlantic waters. Dark Teutonic forests rippled with threat. Sap rose in our American limbs. Our bombers lay waiting, loins tingling with gunpowder, noses toward the future.

Before parting, we made plans to see each other the following evening. I went home and flopped down on the bed and looked up at the ceiling. Something had shifted in the color resolution of my life: there was this new brightness in it, and in contrast to that brightness everything else seemed dim and unimportant. The things that would happen to me between now and the following night—the birthday party I'd attend later that evening, my Sunday library shift—were just interludes, a gray wash of negative space.

That night I could not avoid telling Jimmy about the golden man because he always knows when I've got a love interest I am trying to keep secret. He says that it's right there on my face, that my skin gets red and I go sort of cross-eyed. I don't believe it's that obvious, but somehow he is always correct.

Our friend Samira was turning twenty-eight and had decided to celebrate by cooking Moroccan food for everyone she knew. Like many things Samira did, it was a generous impulse whose execution was hampered by basic, easily predictable facts about reality. Like the fact that she had never cooked Moroccan food before, or that her studio apartment was too small to accommodate everyone she knew, or that her window unit air conditioner would not be able to outperform her stove on even a relatively temperate night in late August. As a result, within twenty minutes of our arrival, Jimmy and I were sitting on her stoop, ordering takeout Thai with an app on my phone while Jimmy smoked a cigarette.

"So I met a new guy," I said, hoping to preempt his needling.

"I thought so. I thought you had that look. Where'd you find this one?"

"The bus stop."

He snickered. "You know, right, that you're just, like, two steps away from picking up a homeless guy under a bridge?"

"Ryan was technically homeless."

"Oh yeah. That was the freegan?"

"Right."

"Where was he living again?"

"Remember? He had a friend who ran an S and M dungeon and he said Ryan could live in the back room, but only if he came out at certain times and opened the dungeon door really abruptly, for people who had a fetish about being interrupted."

"Oh right. Amazing. I can't believe I forgot that." He passed me the cigarette; I took one drag, then passed it back.

"Come to think of it," I said, "I met him at that bookstore in Dumbo, so technically I *did* pick up a homeless guy under a bridge."

This made Jimmy laugh in such a way that he choked on his cigarette smoke, which made us both laugh harder. "Okay," he said. "So what's wrong with this one?"

"He won't tell me."

"What do you mean: you *asked*? I was joking."

I sighed. "I know." So I told him, in detail, about my conversation with the golden man, about the nameless

"bad thing" that had happened to him, his warning about leaving New York, the unexplained excursion to the mailbox.

Jimmy responded with a long, uncharacteristic silence. He stared ahead and frowned. Then he said, "He's married."

"You think so?"

"What else could it be?"

"I don't know."

"Or maybe he's in the witness protection program. Or he just got out of prison! Is he wearing one of those ankle bracelets?"

I groaned.

"Do you know his last name? We could Google him right now."

"No. I didn't, like, ask to see his ID."

"Rach, what if he's a sex offender?"

"He's not a sex offender."

"How do you know?"

"Anyway, I heard that most sex offenders aren't pedophiles or anything. They're people who, like, had sex in a movie theater once, or had sex with a seventeen-year-old when they were eighteen."

"Now you're trying to justify dating a sex offender?"

I stood up, folded my arms. "You're being mean. I'm gonna go back inside."

He looked up at me, narrowed his eyes. "You *really* like this guy," he said.

I looked away. "Maybe," I said. "I don't know yet."

"You do! You really do!" He gave a cackling laugh and made a spidery, anticipatory gesture with his fingers. "Maybe he'll melt your cold, cold heart."

"You know I don't like it when you say that."

"I know. I'm sorry, hon."

I sat down. "You just make me sound so... defective."

"Nobody said you're *defective*. Remember what Samira said that time? You're like a princess in a glass case. You're a little hard to get to. You just have... a different threshold. It's not a bad thing. I mean, would you rather be like *me*?"

He had a good point—I would not have traded places with him—but I still felt it: a familiar hopelessness, like a hollow itching in my gut. Luckily, at that moment our Thai food arrived, and that distracted us both.

"Anyway," I said, after a few mouthfuls, "how's Kit?"

Kit was a man Jimmy had met on Grindr a couple of months before. This was so typical of Jimmy: at the beginning of the summer he had announced that he was done with relationships, that he was Codependent No More, that he was initiating a season of casual assignations untainted by emotion. "I'm calling it SOS," he said. "Summer of Sex." But the second time he met up with a random guy it was Kit, and their date ended up lasting for fifty-six hours. By the time it was over, Jimmy had spent two nights at Kit's property upstate, had FaceTimed with Kit's elderly mother, had spent several hours holding Kit while he sobbed and resolved to finally end his ailing marriage to a modern dancer named Byron who was currently outside Santa Fe in what sounded like a fancy rehab for porn addicts. And this was all before they even had their first butt sex. Anyhow, Jimmy had recently moved into Kit's place, and Kit had immediately discarded all of Jimmy's clothes in secret and bought him all new clothes, for a "fresh start." When Jimmy suggested that maybe this was a teensy bit of an insane thing to do, Kit threatened to kill himself, but Jimmy could tell he hadn't meant it. He was a veteran of people threatening to kill themselves over him and so he had become an expert; he could spot the counterfeit threats like those bow-tied guys on *Antiques Roadshow* can spot a counterfeit Revolutionary War footstool or whatever.

He shrugged. "It's basically the same," he said. "I guess I'm working up the courage to admit how bad it's gotten. I mean, in hindsight it seems so stupid to have moved in." He sighed. "I just thought I was in love. For *real* this time."

"You *were* in love," I said. "Being in love wasn't the problem."

"What was the problem, then?"

"Everything else."

He laughed.

"Seriously, though. Just leave. I'll help you. Because what's next? He already destroyed your clothes. What if he does something to Kierkegaard?"

Jimmy went pale. Kierkegaard was his cat. "I hadn't thought of that," he said.

"Has Franklin found someone else for your old room yet?"

"Yeah, but they can probably kick him out. They don't like him anyway. He keeps making these smoothies and not putting the blender lid on properly, so these little shit-green flecks get all over the kitchen. You know how Franklin is about the kitchen."

"Ugh."

"And he's a *teacher*. Teachers are the *worst*."

"Ask them tomorrow, okay? I'll help you move back. And you can stay with me if you need to."

He elbowed me. "Then where are you gonna fuck your new married sex-offender boyfriend?"

"Shut up."

A window above us opened, and Samira's head emerged. Quickly, we tried to hunch over our takeout trays to obscure her view of them.

"*There* you are!" she cried. "The tagine is almost ready!"

"We'll be up in a minute!" yelled Jimmy. Samira went back inside. We sighed, relieved, and leaned back.

He turned to me. "What do you think the Samira version of a tagine will look like?"

"Who knows? I guess we'll find out."

For a moment, neither of us said anything, but I knew what we were both thinking about: the time Samira had tried to take our whole group of friends on a "secret bike path" through Staten Island that she claimed to have discovered. We'd ended up in some kind of forest that was grown over with nettles and poison ivy and turned out to be some rich person's private property, and one of the rich person's staff people had seen us and called the police. The police officers glanced at our scratched-up, poison-ivy-inflamed legs and weary expressions and took pity on us and gave us a ride back to the ferry in their van. The whole way back to Brooklyn, Samira had talked indignantly about how they definitely, *definitely* would have arrested us if we had all been people of color and not just her and Marcus, who were black, and Flor, who was Filipina. This was probably true but also, in that moment, felt like an annoyingly selective interpretation of our encounter with law enforcement, of her role in bringing it about. Still, this was what we loved about Samira: her determination to insist on her version of the world. We wanted to believe in secret magical bike paths, and improvised Moroccan feasts, and justice: in general, in a world that was more responsive to our imagined visions of it. Yet we hedged our bets. We showed up to her visions with full stomachs, expecting nothing.

Jimmy laid a hand on my leg. "I'm sorry I made fun of your new guy," he said. "I'm sure he's not a sex offender."

"I know."

"Look, if you really like him, don't hold back. I know I'm a bad example, in terms of consequences, but letting yourself free-fall like that? It's the best feeling in the world. I want you to have it."

It always took me aback, how Jimmy could suddenly become sincere like this, out of nowhere. I supposed it was how he seduced people: he teased and poked and got your hackles up, and then, just when you least expected it, he ripped open the door to his gooey boyish heart. I was used to it, but still, in that moment, I felt genuinely touched.

"Thanks, J," I said, leaning my head against his shoulder.

He frowned and sniffed the air. "Do you smell that? Is that smoke?"

I lifted my head from Jimmy's shoulder just as a piercing alarm rang through the air. This was the part of the evening when the friction between reality and Samira's vision of it became so abrasive that something actually caught fire. In this case, it was her entire kitchen. Luckily, some quick-thinking person had immediately grabbed the fire extinguisher and quenched the flames, but coughing people began streaming out of the front door, clutching each other and looking back up at her third-floor window as though at the experience they had just witnessed and escaped. Already they were telling each other about it, as if it had happened a long time ago; already Samira was holding out the singed tips of her long curly hair and announcing her plan to shave it all off to commemorate the experience. Her kitchen mishap had been not a careless mistake but a crucial node in the universe's vast plan for her continuous renewal, a baptism by fire.

Jimmy gave me a smug look and raised an eyebrow; I reciprocated. We generally expected little from other humans besides absurdity. As a result, we were rarely disappointed.

But now, privately, I felt a stab of melancholy: my smoke-free lungs, my full belly, seemed to speak to the kind of defensive wisdom that had always excluded me from the tenderizing blows of experience.

I closed my eyes and thought of the golden man, of his hot hands and crackling eyes, of our date the next day. I would approach it the way Samira would, the way Jimmy-in-love would: inviting risk, entering the dark forest, running back into the burning building in search of my own heart.

Our library is one of only a handful of branches open on Sunday, aside from the big central one, and while I probably should resent this, it's actually a relief; I never know what to do with a Sunday otherwise. There's never anything *to* do, besides brunch: you make conversation for a couple of hours while eating an overpriced omelet you could have made yourself, and then, bloated and drunk from mimosas, you end up sleeping away the afternoon. I much preferred it this way, working busily for a few afternoon hours and then taking a long walk home (my bus did not run on Sundays), feeling the tired tingle in my feet, then curling up with a cup of tea and a pleasure book.

This Sunday, though, it was not the book I looked forward to.

All night and morning, I had thought of the golden man and resisted the impulse to touch myself. This kind of desire was rare and I did not want to squander it. Now I moved around the library in a silent delirium of longing, my outsides taut and awake, my insides tender and molten. I stamped and reshelved books, marveling at how well I could fool everyone: they thought I was a librarian, but I was really a lady volcano.

On my long walk home, I touched everything I could. My desire had expanded outward, to include the whole world. I ran my fingers along chain-link fences, feeling the airy skips between the wires; I laid my palms against the sun-warmed metal skin of the streetlamps. I felt the roughness of tree bark and the pliant tongues of the leaves. I was a body covered in skin, and everything invited my touch.

I'd told Thomas I would cook for him at my apartment, but I am not a very good cook and in my nervousness and sexual agitation I managed to ruin everything except the kale. But when he showed up at my door, his electrical eyes crackling, he was carrying a big fat cherry pie bursting with soft cherry parts, emitting a warm yeasty smell. It was so sensual it was almost pornographic. We both blushed and grew embarrassed when he held the pie between us.

We went up to my roof as the sun set, and ate the kale dripping with garlic and the pie oozing with cherry juice and drank a crisp, sexy white wine. He said that it was the best meal he'd ever had, and I believed him because I agreed.

"Do you cook much?" I asked, licking cherry juice off my fingers.

"Nah," he said. "I mean, I can. But I don't really need to eat that much. Sometimes I just kind of...forget."

"What do you mean, you forget? Don't you get hungry?"

"No," he said. "I sort of graze. I don't need much food."

"But what about your fast circulation? Doesn't that give you, like, a high-octane metabolism?"

He shook his head. "It's not like that. I told you, my body's weird." He paused and frowned, as if he was trying to decide whether to elaborate or not. Instead, he leaned in and kissed me.

The kiss felt just how I had imagined it: a warm welcome shock. I closed my eyes and kissed him back, but then he pulled away and gave me a long, serious look.

"I'm going to be very honest with you right now," he said. "As honest as I can be. Is that okay?"

"Of course," I said.

"You are the first woman I've gone out with in a while," he said. "Like I said, something bad happened to me a couple months back. I don't want to scare you or anything, but this is the first time I've really connected with anybody since then. I still have to leave soon. That's not going to change."

"Uh-huh."

"And I still can't tell you why."

"Uh-huh."

"So if you don't want to get into this, I completely understand."

"Uh-huh."

"But right now I'm really *here*. And I want to be here really badly. I don't want to be anywhere else or think about anything else. I just want to eat pie with you and talk to you and look at your face and touch you everywhere and get your red lipstick all over me."

I considered this for a moment. I let his words sink in. I'd never held any fairy-tale notions of love; I never expected anything to last forever. I had read too many literary novels for that; I understood the nature of the daydream. I just demanded that, like a good literary novel, love be absorbing, and full of texture, and, well, novel. I demanded that it demand something of me.

"Well," I said, "here we are."

He took this as the permission it was, leaned over, and kissed me again—this time deeper, more intentionally, like the sealing of something.

Then we went down to my bedroom and lay on the bed and he touched me slowly, through my clothes. I've always liked this best, the over-the-clothes part. It recalls the illicit feeling of the very first touches I ever experienced, from the nervous hands of older boys, in the backs of school buses and movie theaters and planetariums. I let them cup my tiny breasts in their palms like newborn chicks, but did not grant access to skin. These were the same hands that had touched greasy dollar bills and urinal flush levers all day. But through my clothes I sensed the massive thwarted thrust of their desires and felt both powerful and helpless in the face of such forces, like a person on top of a tall mountain looking up at the stars. Even now I always try to prolong the slow beginning moments, to conjure that lost discovery-channel

AMY BONNAFFONS

feeling. But the guys almost never get it. Their desires move faster than their hands, jumping around in front of them like rodeo clowns, and they get distracted and their hands follow, slapping and clutching at my body as if it might get away.

This man touched me slowly. He seemed confident I would not get away, and his confidence held me in place. He covered my breasts with his palms, warming me through my bra and thin cotton T-shirt. He moved one hand down between my legs and whispered, "I can feel how wet you are." But when he tried to slide a hand into my underwear, I pulled it away, nearly burning myself on his hot wrist.

"Hold on a minute," I said.

I got up and went to the bathroom. My face in the mirror looked like an Impressionist's idea of a face. In the grayish-gold evening light, the edges seemed to blur and fade. I brushed my hair and reapplied my lipstick, then stared at myself until I came back into focus. Then I went to the kitchen and filled two glasses with water, pausing on my way back to look out the kitchen window. The world looked the same as always, like a photograph of itself. It was doing a very good impression of not having changed.

I brought the water back to my room, gave him a glass, and we each took a sip. Then we sat on the bed and looked at each other. Neither of us said anything. I felt his firecracker eyes playing over my skin. Some kind of respiration was happening. The room pulsed like a lung.

"You're so *dense,*" he said, finally. "You're so real."

"'Dense'? 'Real'? Is that your idea of a compliment?"

"Yes," he said. "It's the nicest compliment there is." He set his water down on the bedside table, then reached out and touched my right breast, very very lightly. He leaned in close to my ear. "You belong so well in the world," he whispered. "Fucking you would be like fucking the world."

Then we stood up and removed our clothes, individually and slowly, with a sense of ceremony and purpose. I felt like a virgin bride undressing for her wedding night, or a matador undressing for the sake of donning her ceremonial matador clothes, with all the lacings and flourishes. I was aware of my body as a kind of garment. Or perhaps the awareness *was* the garment. Either way, I stepped into myself. I was aware of how my skin covered me, how it fit so well over my bones and flesh.

We looked at each other. He had my favorite kind of male body: lean and wiry, no extra bulk. His penis was straight and graceful. His skin faintly glowed. "I like it," I said.

"I like yours too," he said. "Holy crap, do I like it."

Then he took a step toward me, closing the distance between us, and embraced me. When he touched me I gave out a little cry: his skin had grown much hotter, and while it wasn't exactly scalding, it was enough to startle me.

He stepped back. "Sorry," he said. "Did I hurt you?"

"It's okay," I said. "I was just surprised. Try again, slower."

He reached out for me again, this time moving oh so slowly through the air, so that even before his skin made contact with mine, I could feel its heat. This gave me the strange sensation that his body extended beyond his skin, and that mine did too: I could feel my beyond-body pulsing into the space between us, touching his beyond-body, greeting it; by the time the skin of his hand actually touched the skin of my shoulder, the touch had already existed, was only building upon itself.

In this way we continued, touching other parts of our bodies with other parts of our bodies, but always slowly, the beyond-touch preceding the actual touch. We did this for hours. While he did not penetrate me, because that seemed like too huge a step to take, I still can't think of any other name for what we did besides "sex." It went on and on with neither of us coming; he couldn't move fast without heating up his body too much, so it was a long slow taffy pull, interspersed with talking and kissing, rather than the wordless, grunting, goal-oriented frenzy I had been conditioned to expect. We fell asleep eventually, around three in the morning, intertwined like children who pass out carelessly, wherever they find their bodies flung midplay. I don't remember falling asleep but

I do remember the feeling I had, a soft orange hum of well-being.

Then, though: the dream.

I dreamed I was underwater, in some kind of river. Above me the sun filtered through clear water, tiny silver fish darting around. Below me lay a riverbed paved with smooth black stones.

I reached down to scoop up one of the stones from the bottom, but the hand that reached down was not my hand. Or actually it *was* my hand—it was clearly attached to me—but it was different: completely stripped of flesh, just an elegant spider of bone. I was a skeleton. I tried to scream, but I was underwater.

I woke up with a start, soaked in sweat. My phone told me it was 4:03 a.m. Thomas was still in my bed, but he'd rolled away from me, curled up on his side facing the wall, the light cotton blanket twisted around him. He looked pale and unreal in the thin, greenish, diluted urban moonlight that streamed through my window.

Still under the spell of the dream, I started to have a strange feeling: that Thomas wasn't there at all, that I had just imagined him, was imagining him now in some kind of waking dream state. I do not mean this as a figure of speech; this is a very real fear of mine, that the things I imagine will take on such solidity that I cannot differentiate them from reality. It is a disease of girls who spend lots of time alone, reading books and making up stories; they grow up to be women with intense dream lives and daydream lives, who sometimes confuse their private reality with the shared reality of others. Sometimes I have referred to something only to see a confused frown on the other person's face, meaning that they have no idea what I am referring to because it never actually happened except inside my head.

I turned on the bedside light, went into the bathroom, and splashed my face with water. When I came back and found Thomas still there, I felt a little bit better. But still some dark thing sloshed around inside me, uneasily; still I was nauseous with the questions the dream had raised, questions that I could not now, in the middle of the night, un-ask.

I suddenly remembered Jimmy's warnings. I hadn't noticed an ankle bracelet, but what if I'd just been distracted? I felt seized by a possessive urge to see his whole body, to confirm his reality, to search the map of his skin for clues that I might have overlooked. Slowly, I slid the comforter down, revealing his sculpted white-gold shoulders. I patted them gently with my hands. They were scalding hot. He didn't wake up. I eased the blanket down further, and then I gasped.

In the center of his chest was a hole the size of a baseball. No blood, no seams, just a perfectly round absence, as if he'd been nabbed by a giant hole puncher. The hole's borders were flesh-colored but fuzzy, like a mirage.

Unsure what to do, I went to the kitchen, poured

myself a glass of water, and drank it in one gulp, standing up. When I got back, the hole was still there.

I eased the comforter down the rest of his body and inspected him thoroughly. No other holes anywhere. No ankle bracelet either.

Now it seemed actually preferable that this was all a dream. The sooner I could wake from it, the better. I went to the bathroom, slugged two mini cupfuls of NyQuil, and returned to the bed. The drug did its work and in a few minutes I'd fallen back into an uneasy, sticky, greenish-colored sleep.

When I woke up in the morning, he was gone.

Over the years, Jimmy and I have developed a habit of texting each other in the middle of the night from strange men's bathrooms. There's always some detail that seems crucial to share—like the stack of old Tintin comics on the back of the toilet tank of the French law student with whom Jimmy had his first threesome; or the way a library school classmate of mine insisted not only on wearing his socks during sex, but on leaving them hitched up his calves like a schoolboy; or the cadence with which a British historian that Jimmy once seduced cried out "Good God!" at the moment of climax.

Eventually these texts acquired a name: "failed novels." "That was one of your best failed novels," we'd say, or "Oh yeah, I remember that detail from one of your failed novels." The truth at the heart of the joke was that Jimmy and I had once been aspiring writers, but realized eventually that we didn't have the stamina to sustain anything for longer than a page. We wrote excellent sentences and paragraphs; our emails were Pulitzer-worthy. But neither of us had ever published anything, or bothered to try.

So our lives became source material for a novel that unfolded in real time, text message by text message. It was like that Joni Mitchell line—"Love is a story told to a friend; it's secondhand." I couldn't truly enjoy the glow of a mounting flirtation, the pleasure of tangling in strange sheets, without describing it. Sometimes the sentences formed themselves inside my head even as the night unfolded, particularly when the date turned out to be cringeworthy: when someone spoke only in pickup-artist clichés, or attempted a sexual move copied inexpertly from porn, or extolled the virtues of paleo or CrossFit. Jimmy could occasionally get swept away: when I didn't get a text, I knew his date had gone well; if it had gone really *really* well, even his later in-person debrief would be hopelessly vague. I occasionally felt bad about this difference between us—about the way I reliably failed to inhabit a moment, instead hovering outside of it, catlike, waiting to isolate and pounce on a tellable detail.

It was only as I surveyed the bedroom that morning, taking in the fact of Thomas's departure, trying to piece together the truth of what I'd seen during the night, that I realized it hadn't even occurred to me to text Jimmy, or to think about the fact that I wasn't texting him. For the first time that I could remember, I'd remained thoroughly within a moment's dreamlike grip; reality had become more potent than a story about it.

Now, this was no consolation. I lay alone in the early-morning light, taking measure of my bedroom's emptiness. The sheets on Thomas's half of the bed were tangled and twisted, as if he'd fled in great haste and agitation. He hadn't left a note.

Last night this space had brimmed over with lovemaking; last night my body had expanded, become a kind of heat, taken up the whole room. Even the corners, even the dark spaces beneath the furniture—it all had been filled. Now the room felt hollow and scraped out.

It had rained during the night, and the woolly light said it was still overcast and drizzly. Everything looked gray and drained of color. I felt as though I was in an old black-and-white movie, perhaps a French or Swedish movie about doomed claustrophobic love, where everyone smokes a lot and makes aphoristic pronouncements about impossibility.

The actress has a beautiful stony face and wears a beret. She holds a cigarette and stares into some vague middle distance to the left of the camera. "He has a hole in his heart," she says. "An actual hole." She reaches down and extinguishes her cigarette with a single cruel motion. End of scene.

The worst part was that I was still turned on. The night before, we'd spent hours working each other up, but neither of us had come. Despite what I'd seen in the middle of the night, despite the room's cold stillborn feeling now, all that potential still hummed in my body. No one had informed certain parts of it, the cave lady parts, of the latest developments. I caught a whiff of his scent on my pillow, and my body responded: urgently, humidly, tropically. This felt grotesquely unfair.

I slid my hand down between my legs and began to vindictively masturbate. I forced myself not to think of him, instead going back to my previous default fantasy, in which I made love to a woman physically identical to myself. I pinned her to the wall and shoved two fingers up her real quick to show her who was boss. Then I tied one of her wrists to the bed and made her touch herself with her other hand. She got really hot from my meanness. Normally this was where things really took off: the moment when the two mes—the objectifier and the object—merged into one being, writhing and squirming in the grip of the same shameful imperative.

But this morning it didn't work. The other me seemed unconvinced. She stared up with a dull, stale look, disappointed, as if to say, *Is this all you've got? And where is the melting, where is the heat?*

I gave up. I needed some coffee. I put the pot on and stared out the window, just as I'd done the day before. Today a veil of fog clung to everything; even from my fourth-floor apartment window, it seemed to coat the lots and backyards. Water above, water below. Water everywhere. I was not in a building but on a ship. Slowly we were pulling away from the dock. Slowly we were leaving reality behind.

Once I got outside, I felt better. Whatever had taken place in my bedroom last night, the outside world seemed unaffected. Real rain fell gently on the heads and umbrellas of real people. I hadn't brought an umbrella myself, a fact I was glad of now. The cool water felt good on my face, a reminder of all the true ways that science described the world. Somewhere clouds were condensing into liquid, gravity pulling the water down. Gravity was a kind of embrace: the earth gathering in the rain, gathering in everything, including me—holding me close to its body, reminding me I belonged.

The other people at the bus stop all seemed soggy and afflicted, coughing into their coat sleeves or staring down at their phones. Thomas wasn't there.

I boarded the bus and, out of habit, watched the waiting area as it pulled away, staring out through the scratched and foggy window at all these people who were not him.

The workday was a wash. I stared off into space, unaware of the library patrons, uninterested even in alphabetizing. All I wanted was to get through my shift, go home, and crawl back into bed. At the same time, bed seemed like the worst, most claustrophobic place to be; my sheets were still tangled and clotted with nightmare.

Halfway through the day, Jimmy texted: how was ur date??? The multiple question marks signaled his surprise at not having received a failed novel about it. I thought a long time before responding. For the first time with Jimmy, I felt tongue-tied: there were English words that existed to describe what I had seen, but when I typed them into my phone and read them back to myself, I felt assaulted by a migraine-like dissonance so profound that I actually had to close my eyes and raise my fingers to my temples and wait for it to pass. In the end I deleted the message and texted it was good but weird...busy day i'll tell u later.

After work I thought about killing time at the coffee shop or bookstore for a while, or taking a walk to tire myself out. But when the bus deposited me back at my stop, I looked across the street and saw that another bus was arriving in the opposite direction—not mine but Thomas's, the one he rode every day. Seized by a sudden impulse, I ran across the street, narrowly avoiding a speeding bicycle, and got on.

I took the same journey I'd taken with Thomas just a few days before, all the way to the end of the line. But this time, of course, I was alone.

When I arrived at my destination, I was disappointed: it was just a normal mailbox, after all. What had I expected? And now that I was here, what was I supposed to do? I looked around, as if for clues, but all I saw was the desolate street and the bus depot on the other side.

At a loss, I opened the little door to the mailbox and stuck my hand in. Nothing happened, but the air was definitely different in there. Colder, and pointier. My hand tingled faintly. Was this simply a consequence of air science? Enclosed spaces, slower movement of oxygen particles? No: after a minute, I got the distinct sense that this air was *doing* something. It was feeling me just as I was feeling it. I'd thrust my arm into a thoroughly active absence. I left my hand in there for a minute or two, letting the air become acquainted with it, and then I slowly pulled it out.

I couldn't really think of anything else to do, but I didn't want to go home yet either. I decided I would leave something behind in the mailbox. It didn't matter what. I held open my bag, rummaged around, and pulled out my notebook, the bus notebook: sometimes I took it out during my ride and jotted down phrases that popped into my mind, or did quick sketches of the backs of people's heads. Now, as I flipped through it, I realized that I hadn't drawn or written anything in the past two weeks. I'd been too busy staring out the window and daydreaming about Thomas.

Annoyed at the notebook's blankness, I opened the little hinged metal door of the mailbox and tossed the entire thing in. Then I crossed the street and took the bus back home.

When I got there, he was sitting on my stoop.

He looked the same as always, wearing his same uniform—except that everything was a shade darker than normal, because he was completely soaked through. He must have been sitting there a long time. Also, his brightness seemed to have dimmed. His eyes still glowed, but flatly, as if tarnished; his hair had lost its luster.

"You're soaking wet," I said.

"I know," he said. "I've been sitting here in the rain." He gave a half smirk, as if he couldn't quite take his own romantic gesture seriously. "The rain," he repeated, holding his hands out to the side, palms upturned. "That's the kind of guy I am. The guy who sits on your stoop in the rain, for hours, just to earn the right to apologize."

I folded my arms. "So," I said. "This is you asking me if you can come in?"

"If you'll have me. I'm sorry. I just want to explain why I left this morning."

I sighed. "It's okay," I said. "Come in, I guess." He followed me inside.

"So," I said. I sat on the couch, looking up at him; he had remained standing, to protect my furniture. Little droplets of water kept falling from his clothes onto the rug.

"So," he said. "Where to begin?"

"I saw your hole," I blurted.

He flinched, as if I'd slapped him, and closed his eyes.

"In the middle of the night," I continued. "I woke up. You were lying there asleep, but you had a giant hole in your chest."

He didn't respond, just stood there with his eyes closed.

"Who *are* you?" I said. "You don't have a cell phone. You won't tell me your last name. You can't reveal anything about your life. And you seem to have...some totally other kind of body."

Slowly, he reached down and peeled up his wet shirt, exposing his stomach inch by inch. Except that where his stomach was supposed to be, I could see right through to the far wall: there was a hole just like the one I'd seen in his chest in the middle of the night, except bigger— and spreading. I watched it expand so far that it almost reached the edges of his body. Only a thin vertical strip of flesh was visible on either side.

"So," he said. "This."

"Yeah. Is this what you meant when you said you were leaving New York?"

"More or less."

"I see now why it was hard to explain. I'd assumed, you know, you meant your whole body at one time."

"Yeah."

"When did it start?"

"Just this morning. I noticed it when I woke up."

"But you knew this was going to happen?"

"Not exactly. But *something* like this. I wasn't surprised. It's hard to explain."

I gazed down at his stomach again—or rather, through it. The wall beyond was covered in wallpaper, a black-and-white vintage-y floral pattern that I'd chosen and put up a week after I moved in, trying to make the apartment's crappiness look artsy and intentional rather than just crappy. It was already starting to peel. I barely noticed it anymore; it had become just another part of the room. But now as I stared at this one patch of it, his flesh surrounding it on four sides like a picture frame, it looked impossibly strange—familiar yet improbable, like a stranger's face that somehow resembled my own. I looked up at Thomas's face, then down at the wallpaper. Face. Wallpaper. Face. Wallpaper.

"Well," I said. "I guess you tried to tell me."

"I did."

"What does it mean?"

He sighed. "As you've probably figured out, I'm not really alive. In the traditional sense."

"What other sense is there? I always thought there was only the one."

"No, there's at least two. I don't know an exact number."

"Were you born like this?"

"No. I was like you once, but I died. 'Died.'" He made exaggerated air quotes, as if it was a silly made-up word.

"How?" I asked.

"I don't want to talk about it. Sorry. Even just thinking about it makes things worse." Sure enough, even as he spoke, the hole slowly expanded. Then I watched the two flesh-colored lines at the edges of the hole completely disappear, so that now he looked as though he'd been cut in half: his chest hovered above his narrow hips, a band of empty space in the middle.

"Sorry," I said. "Are you in pain?"

"No. I don't really even feel my body at all, right now. I'm kind of numb." Slowly, the edges of his abdomen reappeared, and the hole started to contract.

"It was...sudden, wasn't it?" I asked. "Your death."

"Yes." Immediately the hole started to expand again.

"I'm sorry."

"That's okay." He closed his eyes, waiting for his flesh to reclaim the emptiness.

So: this man glimmered so brightly because he was constantly on the edge of not existing. Like anything beautiful on the edge of nonexistence, he now seemed unbearably precious. I didn't care anymore about his disappearance last night. I just wanted to hold him together, and keep him here.

I got up, went into the bathroom, and pulled out my fluffiest towel. Then I went over to him, reached up, and gently began to dry his face and hair. While I did this he looked down at me so tenderly I was afraid to meet his gaze. His hair was curly and soft, like a lamb's, and smelled like wet wool.

After I'd dried his hair, I slowly removed his shirt. He submitted to this disrobing like a child, raising his arms without being asked. Then I wrapped the towel around his narrow shoulders and used its ends to pat down his arms, still glowing faintly. I rubbed down his torso, absorbing the little water droplets from the few sparse hairs on his chest.

"You're so good," he said. "Why are you so good?"

When I reached his stomach, I hesitated. The hole had shrunk, but it was still there, about the diameter of two fists. What would happen if I touched it?

Just then, as if in answer to my question, he lightly took hold of my wrist. I looked up at him. Holding my gaze, he pulled my hand slowly into the hole. I did not resist.

My hand went all the way through, almost up to the elbow. I even saw it come out the other side. I could do a little wave at myself with my fingers. But then my skin started to tingle, the way it had in the mailbox earlier: the air inside the hole was different air. This was an active absence, a force that wanted to know me just as I wanted to know it. No, not just to know me: to take something from me. It corroded and gnawed at reality. The longer I touched it, the further from reality I would move.

So this was what he had inside him. What he'd been battling.

I closed my eyes. It felt important to not remove my hand myself. I would wait for him to do it. I would greet this thing inside of him for as long as it wanted to be greeted. I would extend my hand into the void and give it a firm handshake. I would not be the first to pull away.

He stayed over again that night. Again we spent hours in my room, touching; again I felt melty and open, as if my body had no borders. When my palm touched the warm skin of his arm, when my fingers grazed his inner thigh, when any part of his flesh resisted me and pressed back, I felt keenly aware of its contingency; I might touch him in the same place five seconds later and find nothing there.

In fact, though, he managed to stay together. His hands were there to move over and inside me, his weight was there to hold me down, his penis was there to ask its straight and unmistakable question, and because I felt so open and permeable, the answer was an obvious yes. Still we were careful. We had the slowest, deepest sex, as if everything depended on how carefully we moved, because it did.

During, he made me look into his eyes, despite my impulse to laugh or look away.

"I know how you feel," he said, "because I used to be that way too."

"Looking into someone's eyes like that, it just feels kind of... well, cheesy."

"Think of it as a practical thing," he said. "For me. Looking at you helps me hold together."

"Okay," I said. It had become almost painful to hold his gaze. His eyes were so bright.

"Stay with me," he said. But something was happening in my chest, a gathering pressure that I didn't recognize as a thick knot of tears until it had begun traveling up my throat, full of force and velocity, headed straight for my eyes. By that point I was so off guard that it was impossible to stop it, and soon I was shuddering and he was cupping my wet cheeks and saying, "What's the matter? What's the matter?"

I didn't have a name for the thing that was shaking me as though I might shatter, as though I had already shattered; it was too late, I would never get my old self back. I would never be able to recall its current expansiveness back into its former finitude. I might be condemned to this openness forever.

In my dream that night I lay on a butcher-papered doctor's table in a small examination room. The doctor stood over me, smiling. But he was not dressed like a doctor—more like a fancy old-timey businessman. Impeccably tailored gray suit, light salmon-colored tie, fine silver-rimmed spectacles, black bowler hat, all with a subtle sheen of extreme expensiveness. He had a round white face, smooth features, a well-trimmed goatee.

He smiled. "Have you ever been to Norway?" he asked.

"No, I haven't."

"Magnificent fjords. The very best. I can recommend

a book on the subject: call number 942.13. Watch what I can do with my spine." Then he turned around, and I saw that those finely tailored clothes covered only the front half of his body, as if he was a life-sized paper doll. The reverse side of him was entirely naked, and a zipper ran vertically down the length of his spine, stopping just above his wide flat butt.

He reached behind himself and pulled it down, opening up a hole. As soon as the zipper reached the base of the spine, two hands emerged from the hole, followed by arms and then a head. Slowly a woman came out, freeing herself from the man's body, which collapsed around her like the empty costume it obviously was.

The woman now stood naked in the middle of the pile of shed skin. She looked physically identical to me— exactly as I imagined myself when fantasizing—except that her ears were extra-large, a man's ears, sticking out awkwardly from the sides of her head.

"I didn't mean to be coy," she said. "But I always travel in disguise."

Then she reached up to the sides of her head and, with one vigorous yank, ripped her ears off. Blood started gushing out of the holes, but her facial expression didn't change at all. She held the bloody ears out to me as an offering. "I believe these belong to Dr. Moon," she said. "If you'd be so kind as to pass them along."

"Who's Dr. Moon?" I asked.

She didn't answer. I sat up on the table, the butcher

paper crinkling and rustling beneath me. I held out my hands and she placed the two bloody ears into them, open side up. They were lightly glazed with fine golden hairs. They glowed faintly in my hands.

"But these look like Thomas's," I said.

She gave a thin smile. "My blood runs outside of me now," she said softly. "Where it belongs."

I looked down at the pool of blood forming on the floor. It was spreading outward. When it reached the base of the table, it began to climb, flowing against gravity, inching up the leg. It was coming for me. I gasped.

The other me giggled softly. "It's gonna help you, silly," she said. "You need a blood transfusion. You're dying. That's why you're here."

The blood was traveling along the edge of the table now, about an inch from my thigh. "Let it embrace you," she whispered. "It's thicker than water. It's life."

"What about you?" I cried. "Won't you die?"

She didn't answer. Her smile faded, or turned into a different kind of smile, no longer playful. She smiled through an infinite sadness, like a faded saint in a medieval painting. "You're such a stupid little hermit crab," she said. "In such a stupid, stupid, stupid little shell."

"I thought I was a sea urchin," I said.

Before she could answer, the blood reached me. Just before it touched me, it congealed into the form of a hand. Then the hand reached up and grabbed my thigh, and I screamed.

"What?" said Thomas. "What is it?"

I was still screaming, still half in the dream. Slowly his face came into focus. I felt the weight of his body straddling mine, the pressure of his hands against the sides of my face. "Shh," he said. "It's all right."

I closed my mouth, looked up at him. "You're missing your ears," I observed.

He raised his hands to the sides of his head, where his ears should have been, and set his mouth in a stoic line. "Don't worry," he said. "They'll come back." He rolled off me and sat up.

"In my dream," I said, "I was supposed to give your ears back to you. My doppelgänger had them." I sat up next to him, reached over, and touched the sides of his head. I could feel that faint tingle, that corrosive effervescence of absence. Then I touched my own ears, solid and warm. I imagined cutting them off and plugging them into his head. But they would just be rejected, like mismatched organs. I was made of different stuff from him.

I'd never felt so trapped inside my own separateness. I returned my hands to the absence of his ears, playing my fingers across their invisible rims as if across rosary beads, patiently awaiting the slow tingle of their re-becoming.

Then: three weeks of nocturnal geothermal explorations and hazy half-awake days. Every morning, when I left for work, I left him naked in my bed; when I got home, he was already there, waiting (I had given him a key). Every night we stayed up as long as possible, testing our respective limits: his structural integrity, my capacity for withstanding high temperatures. For a while, we pulled through like champions: there's nothing to boost your sexual adrenaline like a rapidly draining hourglass hovering above the bed.

Then, though, we began to lose the race against time, or against death, or whatever other force was pulling him apart. His molecules barely held together; he'd seem fine and then, just like that, they'd come apart like loose shoelaces. His body would untie from itself, and a hole would open up. I'd try to place my palm on his taut, resistant stomach, and instead nothing would resist me; I'd feel air, then the cool sheet beneath him. Sometimes it was his arm or chest that vanished. Once his head: I was kissing him and then I just pitched forward, my tongue curling and wagging through empty space. When these unravelings happened, he said, he still felt me, in a secondhand way, like watching a movie of someone being touched.

His molecules would always eventually come back together, but when they did, they'd move faster than normal, and his body grew hotter than ever. Several times I burned myself. After one night with him I had to soak my hands in a bowl of ice water. Once I woke up with an actual scar, a fuzzy stripe across my inner arm. We learned to sleep with a flannel sheet between us, for safety.

His penis would become especially hot, a baton of dense flame. If we used lots of lube, I could stand it. In fact the pleasure depended upon the pain, the way certain thick sunsets depend upon smog. He moved so slowly inside me, to minimize friction that might generate more heat. I loved it. People talk about feeling their insides melt, but only I knew what that actually felt like. I was the only woman who had ever melted in this particular way. When I thought of a regular lukewarm penis now, it seemed so boring, like an old wet sock.

We might as well have been the first man and the first woman: risking everything, learning the limits of the body, figuring everything out from scratch.

Of course it was impossible to tell anyone about any of this. What language would I have used? I myself knew very little of Thomas's past, only what it had shaped him into: someone incandescent and voluble, with depths carved out by suffering and a reckless commitment to pleasure.

As it happened, I managed to avoid seeing any of my friends in person for nearly a month. This was shockingly easy. In New York City, it is possible to disappear with very little effort. Even though hundreds of people see you every day, most of them don't know you, wouldn't miss you. The people who do know you are busy and exhausted and assume you are too. Plus, at least half of my friends were professional flakes, and even in the best of times I had a habit of sometimes ignoring them and going into private Rachel worlds for weeks at a time— so my actual life turned out to be the perfect alibi. Like a camouflaged lizard, I hid in plain sight.

As for my family, I took their calls as I always had, answered their questions as cryptically as usual. It was pointless to tell my parents about a boyfriend unless they were likely to meet him at Christmas; I hadn't mentioned a man to them in years. (They sometimes asked me how my old boyfriend Mark was doing, even though they knew I hadn't seen him since college; this was as close as they ever came, in their Wasp-polite way, to accusing me of lesbianism or premature spinsterhood.) As for my much older sister, she was a narcissist and thus easy to lie to.

If I had not been so caught up in the daydream, it might have alarmed me, how easy it was to shed or distort these connections upon which my life as a social being depended. But I didn't have time to think, any more than an athlete has time to think while running a triathlon. I was attempting the impossible: sustaining a fragile daydream through the power of my fucking, through sheer force of will.

I could not entirely avoid Jimmy. But Jimmy had problems of his own: the night after my second sleepover with Thomas, Kit's husband, Byron, had finally returned from rehab; as it turned out, he and Kit had *not* come to a crystal clear understanding about the nature of their relationship, specifically the fact that it was over. This had become apparent when Byron had opened the door in the middle of the night and yelled "Where the fuck were you? I had to take a cab from fucking Newark!" and then "Who the fuck is that?" and then "Oh no, you motherfucker, not again."

A fight had ensued, a fight whose contours might at first have seemed predictable but soon became less like a fight than like a Charlie Kaufman film: just when you thought you understood the genre you were in, it swerved and gained a sudden self-awareness and under-mined itself and became something else entirely. I'll spare you all the twists and turns and just say that by the time the sun rose, several expensive objects had been threateningly brandished, including a broken bottle of Bordeaux and the blunt end of a Buddha statue; each of the three had, at one point or another, sobbed from the sheer force of sudden self-revelation; and finally, they had all had sex together, sex that was enhanced by Byron's long-standing porn addiction and the pressure cooker of his seventy celibate days. By the time they went out for brunch at 2 p.m. the next day, they were a throuple.

Jimmy had never been a member of a throuple before; learning the rules and nursing his partners' fragile egos and attending several therapy sessions a week absorbed all of his attention. Thus, conveniently little was required of me as a friend besides responding to his frequent texts and infrequent phone calls and supplying the ap-propriate exclamations of astonishment or excitement or sympathy. He did ask about me, but it was easier than usual to give an evasive half answer and steer him back to himself.

So the rest of my life continued—technically. Septem-ber had arrived; school had started. The library was quiet during the day again. But nothing in daily life was a match for the heat and terror of the daydream, which had

finally found a place to thrive: in the shimmering negative space opened up within Thomas's body, between his
body and mine. It did not surprise me that the daydream
had required, or occasioned, a tear in the fabric of reality.
I had never underestimated its strength.

But I was also learning that there was, in fact, another
force strong enough to compete with the daydream: fear.
Every time a hole opened up in his body, I felt the daydream waver and jump like firelight. On the other side
of the daydream lay not what had been there before—
my boring, ordinary life—but its shadow, a yawning
blackness, a territory I had never even come close to
encountering. If and when he did disappear, in some final
way, how would I continue? How could I carry this dark,
unshareable knowledge? Could a person even remain a
person, after such intimacy with death?

I'm not an idiot. I *knew* how crazy it was, what I was
doing. And yet, and yet—even with only the barest, most
partial knowledge of his life (I still didn't even know his
last name), I felt confident in applying the word "love" to
what was happening between us. I'd been a goner since
he'd pulled my arm through his stomach there in the
middle of the carpet, since I'd felt his death lick my hand
with its prickly tongue, since I'd become the keeper of
his secret.

This love required a certain kind of mystery, the
way a fire required oxygen. Deprive it of that oxygen

and it would die—perhaps not completely, but it would die down into something ember-like, something barely there, something whose warmth offered the memory of flame rather than flame itself. So, as unbelievable as this may seem, I hadn't asked him to explain anything.

On the one hand, I wanted to know everything about him; I wanted no part of his life to remain foreign or inaccessible. Even the air that touched him had become precious to me. On the other hand, I knew my myths, and they all said you could kill something by seeing it too clearly. Cupid and Psyche shared a perfect love, but only in the dark. Plagued by doubt, she raised a lamp to his face; he disappeared.

Each hole that opened up in Thomas's body was one more hole we might fall through and never come back up again. But as long as he had enough of a body for me to hold—as long as he had warm skin to press against mine—the risk seemed worth it. I could only hope that whatever force was dissolving him from the inside out wouldn't eventually dissolve me too.

Sometimes I thought about Thomas as a person who'd been alive, in a normal way, before. I imagined him belonging to other people: parents, co-workers, friends, lovers. He was not just the solitary golden man who'd inhabited my bed for weeks—he was a glittering shard of a larger story, cut loose and drifting, surrounded by an ache of negative space.

And me? After being less than nothing to him—
a stranger—a month before, I'd become his entire new
reality; I'd become reality itself. "You're so *dense,* you're
so real," he'd said on our first night together. "Fucking
you would be like fucking the world."

Perhaps this is, on some level, what every woman
longs for: the chance to become the world for another
person, to prove that she is a world. I felt this urge
ripening inside of me as we lay curled together on the
bed. It seemed like a worthy use of my life. I mean, what
else had I been planning to do with it?

At the same time: where did it end? What if the world
I lived in, the world for which I'd come to stand in, was
already in some way lost to me?

One night, the entire lower half of Thomas's body disappeared while he was inside me. I could still feel him, like a minty tingle spreading through my loins, but with no weight or pressure.

We took a break and waited for his missing flesh to reappear, but even after it did, the sex felt different. He was spooked. He fucked me aggressively, as if he'd forgotten about me—as if I wasn't even there, as if the purpose of the fucking was to prove he had a penis, to prove that his penis was stronger than death. He fell asleep instantly afterward, his head conking back on the pillow like a thousand-pound weight, and began to snore.

I lay next to him, wide awake, my blood thumping, my vagina raw and sore. I'd had this feeling before, with other men, this feeling of being a receptacle. But Thomas I could forgive: he was fighting a losing battle, and even if my body occasionally had to serve as its scuffed battleground, he was fighting it *for me*.

He loved me. He loved me. I repeated this in my mind now, lying next to this snoring man who was, let it be known, willing to literally cheat death, to risk hell, to remain in my company. How many women I knew could say that of their easy boring sex-only-on-the-weekend boyfriends, with their bank accounts and their carpentry hobbies and their anxieties about marriage? None, that's how many. Zero.

I curled up next to him and stroked his sleeping chest, rising and gently falling, and felt a big zero surround us like a halo, or like a noose—tightening around us, encircling us in its ominous glow.

The next day was Friday. I was yanked into consciousness around eight o'clock, reluctantly, by the drone of Thomas's snoring. Usually he woke with me—usually, in fact, he was the one to nuzzle or lick me out of my sleep, like a hungry cat. I sat up and looked at him. I'd never seen him sleep this deeply.

Alone in the kitchen, I made coffee, ate a bowl of Cinnamon Toast Crunch, tried to read a graphic novel, but my gaze kept drifting out the window. My mind kept playing and replaying the events of the previous thirty-six hours. Thomas had taken up so much of my life in the past month or so, had *become* my life to such an extent, that I barely knew what to do with myself when I wasn't with him. I hardly had my own brain anymore.

I picked up my phone and reluctantly scrolled through the messages. There were a couple from Samira and Flor, asking me if I was coming to a mutual acquaintance's housewarming brunch that weekend. I couldn't bring myself to respond to either of them. I'd already ignored an earlier call and several texts from Jimmy. The last one said Situation deteriorating fast over here ... K found porn in B's browser history, B accused K of spying, I accused of "enabling," F says N not leaving ... help? Reading this text, I felt nothing but an annoyance so sharp it bordered on disgust. I couldn't bring myself to care about Byron's histrionics, and I couldn't even figure out who F and N were supposed to be.

I tried to consider my friends more deliberately, to imagine a way back to them, but I couldn't seem to muster the will. I had no attention to spare for others; I couldn't hope for their comprehension, and I didn't need their sympathy.

I'd dated unadvisably before—the long-distance architect, the married whiskey distiller, the homeless freegan, the philosopher who'd recently broken an eight-year vow of celibacy. During these brief relationships I'd had to endure a certain facial expression from Flor and Samira and sometimes even Jimmy: their brows knitted in concern, their eyes dark with doom foreseen. *I don't care*, I kept wanting to scream. *I know you're concerned for my heart, but I'm not entirely sure I have one, not in the same way as other people. That hard little fist in my chest, it won't ever completely unclench. So what if I tempt fate?*

Now, for the first time, I'd met my match. Complementary weirdnesses. The cratered moonscape of his body. The moony craters of my mind.

I went back to the bedroom and found Thomas still

asleep, still in the same position—curled up on his side like a comma, clutching a pillow. Absurdly, I envied the pillow. I climbed in next to him and began to stroke and kiss him awake.

"Mmm," he croaked. Murmur of pleasure or protesting groan? I didn't care anymore. I eased him onto his back and climbed on top of him. I straddled his hot hips, feeling his straight hip bones press into my soft thighs. He was half hard but still half asleep, murmuring nonsense words, his eyes fluttering open and then closed again. I kissed his neck and slowly rocked my pelvis back and forth, feeling him stiffen beneath me.

"Good morning!" I said.

I arched back and reached down and pulled him inside of me. His penis was scalding; I sucked my breath in and let it out slowly.

"Oh God," he said. "I don't know if I can do this right now."

"You *can*. It's just me. Doesn't it feel good?"

"It feels good," he said. "It always feels good. I always want you." But he closed his eyes again, as if in pain.

I rode him harder and faster. His penis reached up inside of me, higher and higher, but the rest of him lay flat on the bed. He tossed his head from side to side and lightly moaned but otherwise lay inert, simply letting me fuck him.

I cried out, shuddered, collapsed, felt him spurt and wither inside of me, flopped down next to him on the bed. I looked over at him. His mouth was open, his eyes closed. He appeared unconscious.

"Are you *asleep?*" I asked. He didn't answer, but then something started to happen, something that hadn't happened before: his entire body flickered, like a strobe light—on-off, on-off, there-gone, there-gone. For a second I thought, *I've killed him. My sex has killed him, my monstrous desire. What have I done?*

I knelt beside him and gave him a series of light slaps on the cheek. "Come back to me, Thomas," I whispered. "Come back." Gradually, he did: the pulse of his disappearing slowed down, the gaps between his absences widened, and finally it seemed as though he was all there again.

He opened his eyes and looked at me and said, "I'm sorry. I'm sorry. I'm just so *tired.*" Then he closed his eyes again. This time, I let him go.

I dialed work and told them I was sick. While Thomas slept, I panic-cleaned my apartment, scouring the windows and bathroom tiles in a flurry of fearful remorse, using six or seven Swiffer cloths for each room, convinced that if I only liberated my home from every last speck of dust, I might free myself from this sludgy feeling of wrongness, the feeling that I'd taken things past some inevitable crisis point, waded into the swampy sucking territory of no return.

I was so furiously absorbed in my task, crouched in the corner of the living room to swab dust from the baseboards, that I didn't feel Thomas enter the room, come up behind me, crouch down; I just suddenly felt his warm hands on my ass, his stomach on my back, and then he was enveloping me, pulling me backwards onto his lap. I fell into him with relief. He kissed the side of my neck. "I'm awake now," he said. "I think I'm better."

"I'm sorry about before," I said. "I was scared. I'm not used to—"

"Don't apologize," he said. "Don't be a downer. Please? I'm feeling good right now. I want to keep feeling good."

I turned around, cupped his face in my hands. "Listen," I said. "Let's go outside. Let's go do something. Eat pancakes or fried pickles. Go to Coney Island."

There was a moment of hesitation—a moment when I saw the question flicker across his face, the *What will happen if?*—but then he smiled, and took both my hands, and pulled me up to stand. "Go put on your nicest dress, Rachel Starr," he said. "We're going out."

The nicest dress I owned was my bridesmaid dress from my sister's wedding. It was green satin, with a scalloped bodice and a wide tulle skirt. It was a little too chilly now to wear *only* the dress so I covered it with an old tweed blazer.

"You look like Miss Havisham," he said. "Or like a homeless debutante."

"Do you like it?"

"I love it."

We practically ran down the stairs of my walk-up, then flagged down a green Boro taxi without discussing where we were going. "Brighton Beach," I told the driver, then looked over at Thomas for confirmation. He nodded in approval.

The whole taxi ride, we were too nervous to simply rest; we drummed each other's palms, spidered our fingers up each other's arms. I kept shifting around, the green satin of my dress moaning against the coarse imitation leather of the seats. He jiggled his leg. Already the trip had a manic Hail Mary energy, a frantic limit-pushing glee.

We got out at Brighton 6th Street, in front of a big Russian grocery store that had a suited attendant who removed your bags from you when you entered, giving you a thick plastic baggage claim ticket. We toured the island of steaming prepared foods, royal-purple cabbage and fragrant pierogies and blood-colored borscht and the robust steamy balls of potatoes; we marveled at the meat counter, where a sullenly made-up teenage girl, eyes shadowed and mascaraed as if for a dance club rather than a butchery, sliced us thick bright-red portions of sausage. Here were the iridescent red jewels of wrapped candy, here the thick stinky flesh of fish. Here the dark cherries and imported chocolate, the thick buttery almond-laden cakes. Here was bounty, abundance.

We filled our grocery cart, then walked with heavy plastic bags to the beach. We sat down and spread the food out before us, swatting the seagulls away, not worrying about the sand in our shoes. We ate until we were ready to burst, then lay back on the beach. He took off his jacket and made a tent of it above our faces, and we kissed in the sudden dark.

"I don't regret anything," he said.

"Me neither," I said. "Who said anyone regretted anything?"

"No one," he said. "I'm just saying."

"Okay, okay."

After we'd kissed and dozed for a while, succeeding at losing track of time, we removed the jacket from above our heads to discover that the world had changed unwelcomely. The sun was low in the sky now, half gone behind the cauldron rim of the ocean. In the last half hour the world had tilted toward darkness. Everything was chilly and metallic, the stored-up sunlight gone out of things, the shadows long across the grayish-beige sand.

We didn't say anything. We just got up, shivering, rubbing our arms. The big Russian lunch sat in my stomach like cement. Or perhaps something else sat there, a thick gray slab of undigestible feeling. Either way, I felt so heavy I could barely walk.

We dumped our leftovers in the garbage can, disgusted by the half-eaten sight of them: the hardened cave of the whitefish salad, the briny waste of the pickled peppers, the crusty rims of the bread. Then we walked to the subway, silent, arms folded, bodies contracted into themselves for warmth. On our way I looked around for cabs, but there were none to be seen; they didn't roam this neighborhood at this time of night. We were on our own.

We swiped our MetroCards and sat on the bench to wait for the train. Thomas kept looking around the subway platform nervously, though no one else was there—as if one of the shadows might suddenly leap out and seize him.

I took his hands in my lap and held them between mine. He didn't resist, but he didn't say anything either; he just gave me a tight half smile and then went back to darting his eyes around the platform. One of us, I felt, had to say something. One of us had to perform the necessary distractions.

"Did I ever tell you," I asked, "about my first-grade teacher, Mr. Goldberg?"

"Who?"

"Mr. Goldberg. My first-grade teacher. In our school, each class was required to put on a class play once a year. Most of them did, like, Stone Soup or something like that. But Mr. Goldberg was this big opera buff, and every year his first graders put on an opera. Condensed, of course, and they just lip-synched along to recordings of the arias. But real operas. My year we did *Tosca*."

"I'm no expert, but isn't that pretty dark?"

"Yeah. Of course she kills herself at the end. Mr. Goldberg told us that all the best operas have a big loud lady who kills herself. Maggie Glenn was the lead, and at the end she jumped off the stage and kind of collapsed onto the auditorium floor. Goldberg had to teach her how to jump in a way that looked like falling but was still safe. You know, lawsuits—are you okay?"

He'd started to shake noticeably. "Yeah," he said, trying to sit up straight. "I'm just tired."

"I know," I said. "We'll get you home soon. Look, here comes the train." Its headlights were rounding the bend in the track, the long metal snake of its body following behind.

We got on, blinking and shielding our eyes against the painfully bright fluorescent light of the train car, then found a seat.

He closed his eyes, then opened them again. "Keep telling the story," he said. "About Mr. Goldberg."

"Okay," I said. "Well, I was in the chorus, of course, because—oh my God." He had suddenly started to flicker—not all of him, thank God, but the worst part: his eyes. The rest of his face was intact, but his eyes blinked on and off, there-gone, there-gone, like bad Christmas lights.

This had never happened before. These black holes in his head were more terrifying than any of his previous unravelings. He leaned over, his head between his legs. I lunged to cover his body with my body, then took off my jacket and covered his head.

Then I looked up and saw what he'd been looking at: a

poster on the subway wall, right at our eye level, in which a Nordically good-looking blond man in a leather jacket points a gun right at the viewer, his blue eyes narrowed in some kind of photogenically badass emotion. Underneath him were the words THOR HALVARSSON, and in smaller letters below that MALE MODEL, HIRED GUN. It was an ad for a movie, probably a made-for-TV one; Thor Halvarsson's flawless face was generic and unfamiliar. But his gun looked real, pointed directly at you, its dark barrel like an empty eye, its blunt gaze accosting you, accusing you of your killability.

Was this a clue about his death? This flinching at the poster? I closed my eyes and imagined all the scenarios that might have involved a gun. We were Americans, in the early twenty-first century, and there were so many possible variations. School shooting? Drive-by? Hunting accident? Gunned down in a movie theater, in an airport, on a bus? I wanted to know. I wanted to picture it: who had held the gun, who else had been there, where he had been hit, how he had crumpled and bled, who he might have held or who might have held him. I wanted to hold that memory with him, for him, so that he didn't have to hold it all by himself.

Maybe it hadn't been a gun. Maybe there had been no weapon. Maybe he was responding to what the gun represented: death itself, the same menace always, no matter its disguise. There were so many different kinds of accidents, so many ways the body could collide with harder or sharper things, so many vulnerabilities nestled even *within* the body, like land mines. The entire body was an Achilles' heel.

It occurred to me, eventually, that he could put on my sunglasses and close his eyes and pretend to be blind, and I could guide him by the elbow all the way home. So that's what we did. We exited the subway and walked back to my apartment, he in my cat-eye prescription sunglasses, me holding on to him and whispering our route. His deathliness remained undetected; we had averted the worst. But I could feel him bristling under my hand, desperate to get home, resentful at being forced into this public admission of defeat.

That night, we didn't have sex. Exhausted, he fell asleep as soon as he hit the pillow; I lay awake longer, turning the day's events over and over in my mind, then finally drifting into a restless, prickly slumber.

The next morning, I woke up feeling the itchy, ominous kind of uneasiness you feel when you know you've forgotten to do something but can't remember what. Thomas was still sleeping, so I decided to go for a walk. I wrote a note: *Gone out 11am, back soon, R.*

As I left the building, I suddenly realized I was ravenous, which came as a relief: my hunger might give purpose to my wanderings. I could go to Brooklyn Provisions and return with unnecessarily fancy sandwiches, or perhaps a wheel of cheese and some rosemary crackers—

something to affirm our bodies' material instincts, to remind us that there was more than one reason to feel good about being alive.

But as soon as I entered the store, I froze in my tracks: someone had spoken my name.

"Rachel!" said the voice again. I turned in its direction. It was Samira. She'd been standing right by the door, by the refrigerated case holding designer sodas and kombucha; the only reason I hadn't recognized her was that her hairstyle was different. Instead of the long corkscrew curls, her hair was now cut short, forming a black cloud around her face. In a rush I remembered the kitchen fire, the singed tips of her hair; I recalled that I hadn't seen her since then.

"Oh my God!" she cried, embracing me. Samira was known for her ardent, clutchy hugs; they always made me feel both affirmed and vaguely oppressed. Weakly I moved my arms around to her back, gave it a half-hearted pat. I felt my heart pounding against my ribs.

"It's been *forever*!" she murmured, releasing me and holding me at arm's length, searching my face. "Where have you *been*? Are you going to Claire's brunch? That's where I'm heading now—I told her I'd bring a baguette."

"Oh," I said, pulling away. "No. I can't go. I have... another thing."

She folded her arms. "Jimmy told me you have a new guy."

"Yeah...well." I felt myself blushing. "It's been kind of intense."

"Intense how? When do your friends get to meet him?"

It would have been easy to make up an excuse, but I found myself speechless. Looking into Samira's face, its wide-open candor, was doing something to my insides—making them quiver as though I'd burst open from the middle. I froze in place, immobilized by the presence of alien warmth, trying to still my trembling long enough to respond to her question.

Samira's warmth should not have been alien; it was deeply familiar to me, a specific warmth I'd known since our freshman year of college—since we'd whispered from adjacent sleeping bags on our orientation hike, giggled while squatting together behind a bush. Why was it so threatening now?

She reached out again and laid a hand on my arm. "Are you okay, Rach? You look kind of—"

I didn't hear the end of her question; I had already whirled around and pushed my way out the door. I found myself sprinting back toward my building, my thin Keds slapping the pavement clumsily, trying to outrun the feeling her concerned gaze had provoked.

The problem was, Samira knew me so well: I couldn't fake her out, and I couldn't tell the truth. Until that moment, it hadn't been clear to me just how far I'd drifted from my previous reality, how impossible it would be to connect that reality to this new one, in which a dead man lay waiting for me in my bed.

I rounded the corner at the end of my block, slowed

to a lopsided trot and then a walk. Finally I stopped in front of my building and sat down on the stoop.

I supposed I was getting exactly what I'd asked for: I'd been consigned to the daydream, forced to see its terrible unfolding all the way through. Perhaps this was Fate: the thudding inevitability contained like a dark seed at the heart of our most private desires. It lay dormant until something coaxed it awake; once awoken it grew riotously, choking and overtaking all previous paths.

I tried to breathe deeply and stay in place. My heart was pounding—from the run or from the fear, I couldn't be certain. I felt my phone buzz in my pocket. It had to be Samira, asking me what had happened, seeking to confirm my okayness. I let the phone go on buzzing, then die: I couldn't confirm anything for anyone. Finally I let out a long exhale and made my way back up the stairs.

After that, of course, things could hardly get better. Thomas was permanently spooked, like a skittish horse: doom-nettled, frantic-eyed, haunted. I was hardly better myself, though I succeeded in maintaining a surface calm. We almost never left my apartment. Actually, he didn't leave at all, worried that someone would see him in his disintegrating state. He never said so, but I knew. It was unclear which he feared more: the stares of human passersby or some otherworldly repercussion, one he lacked the language to explain.

Each day, his dissolution accelerated visibly; he grew porous as Swiss cheese; he was increasingly more absent than present. I left only to work or get provisions, racing back home as soon as I could, hoping to find him still there. Our every interaction was a game, a race against his body. When he had a stomach we stuffed ourselves with food. When he had a penis I sucked it into a rifle. When he had a tongue he kissed me so deep it was as if he was planting seeds inside of me, pushing them into the dark loam of my throat, hoping to burrow some part of himself into my living flesh.

But mostly we waited. Mostly he was too tired to do

anything else. It took a lot of energy to hold himself together, even partially. At night we'd lie on our backs on the bed, a thin strip of space between us, like husband and wife mummies. He slept or half slept, conserving energy, trying to stay this side of nowhere. But I, I, I: I was a thin blade of somethingness, and I'd never wanted him worse. I lay next to him, aching and aflame, remembering the last times he'd touched me, fantasizing about when he'd touch me next, scheming my way out of the knowledge waiting for me like so much unopened mail.

On my days off I sat in bed with him, holding his hand, or whatever part of his body was available to me at that moment, and we watched movies or I read out loud to him or stroked his head in my lap while I listened to him fret: "What's going to happen to me? What's going to happen to *you*?"

It was already clear that in some way, by joining my body with this warm-fleshed ghost's, I had at least placed my toe on the line between life and death. I might even have crossed it. Death had penetrated me. I had penetrated death. At night I continued having strange dreams—swimming through that river paved with black stones, or seeing myself walk blindfolded through a dark forest, or watching my earless double drip rivers of blood.

And those were just the visions that belonged to me. Now I had also begun to dream of his death, but image-lessly: just a deep darkness, then a scream like a gash through the air. When I woke up from these dreams and saw him sleeping there next to me, oblivious to the journey I'd just taken through his memory, I knew that even though he had in some way survived it, in other ways he was still trapped in that moment—even when he was walking or sleeping or eating or making love, he would always be flinching in response to that scream. If my body might occasionally muffle it, provide him insulation, give him the illusion of safety—well, that was purpose enough for me, for now.

And as for the rest of my life? I tried not to think about my friends, but sometimes I couldn't help it. I'd sent vague, placating texts to Jimmy and Samira and Flor, but I knew I couldn't hold them off much longer— eventually they would stage some sort of intervention, or desert me completely. The two possibilities were equally unthinkable. *Just wait*, I silently pleaded. *Just wait until I get to the other side of this, whatever that looks like. Just wait until I see whether there's anything left of me then. Please don't give up on me yet.*

One day, back at the library—in fact, I remember exactly what day it was; it was September twenty-ninth, my mother's birthday—I was going through a stack of books to reshelve, organizing them by call number, when one of the numbers jumped out at me for some reason. The call number was 942.13.

I frowned: *942.13.* Why did that number sound familiar? Then I remembered: this was the number that the strange man had cited in my dream about the hospital room and the bloody ears, the dream I'd had the second night Thomas stayed over.

I picked up the book. It was called *Fjords of the World: A Compendium.* I flipped briefly through it. It was an old book with a cloth cover, frayed and finger-oiled, falling apart at the edges. All of the illustrations of fjords were drawn in ink, in a careful, crabby hand. My eye alighted on a random phrase: *Fjords can penetrate the earth very deeply. Norway's Sognefjord extends more than four thousand feet below sea level.*

"Have you ever been to Norway?" the man had asked me. At this point nothing really surprised me anymore. I didn't know how or why it had found me, this book, but

I knew—the way you just *know* things—that I had to get home, immediately.

I called out some excuse to Tanya and Jo-Ann and ran outside, flagging down a green taxi instead of waiting for the bus. When the car screeched to a halt in front of my building, I threw a twenty at the driver without checking the fare, slammed the door, and went inside.

I ran up the stairs to my apartment and then stopped short, breathless, on the fourth-floor landing. The silence was deafening. Something loosened and dropped inside of me, like an elevator cut from its cables. Frantic now, I pulled out my keys and fidgeted open the door.

I yelled Thomas's name as I entered, but just as I'd feared: no response. I walked through the apartment looking for him, calling his name just in case, but of course there was no one there. No one in the bed, no one beneath it. No one on the couch or in the kitchen. No one on the toilet or under the sink. Just me, and my apartment, and the vacuum that had opened up in my life.

He was gone. Whatever world he'd come from had finished reclaiming him. And along with him, it had claimed some part of me.

I lay down on the bed and curled up. I'd been half expecting this moment to come, but I couldn't accept that it had finally arrived. I couldn't believe it had happened without me. When I'd allowed myself to think about it,

I'd pictured this kind of tearful deathbed scene, his body lying on top of mine and fading away slowly, both of us crying while he pointillistically disintegrated. My body would be the last thing his body touched in this world. Just imagining it now, in his absence, I felt tears welling up; I shut my eyes hard, to hold them in.

But just when I felt them hot behind my eyeballs, just when I was about to open my mouth and let out a wail, I stopped. I sensed someone's presence in the room.

I opened my eyes and looked around. No one was there. In the gray twilight, the bed was a moonscape of tangled sheets and emptiness. But then I felt him.

Well, not *him* exactly. That tingle, the one from the mailbox and the holes in his body? It was suddenly on top of me, covering my whole body, everywhere. The tingles moved tighter and faster over certain areas, and I intuitively understood that he—or his absence, his shadow— was touching me in those places. A man-shaped absence, equal to him, was straddling me, holding my arms, nuzzling my neck.

In case you've never made love with an invisible person before, and I'm guessing you haven't, let me tell you what it's like. It's amazing. Obviously, he didn't have any body parts, but I sensed where he was by the location and the pressure of his touch. In response, my hands moved over and through him. Then he was inside me, his absence was making love to me. I was fucked by the void.

It was already so much better, now that he didn't have

a body. I could sense, in the ease with which he moved over me, that he felt joyful and free, that he wasn't in pain anymore. He was no longer killable; he had no body left to kill. No one could find him because there was nothing left to find.

Plus, we had no secrets anymore. How can someone who does not have a mouth keep a secret? It's an oxymoron. Or that's the wrong word, but you know what I mean. By altering what honesty meant, we had made a new kind of honesty possible.

It turns out that an absence can penetrate you much more thoroughly than a presence. As he moved inside and on top of me, the tingles worked their way through me, so that I felt them not just in the places he was actually touching me but all through my body. My bloodstream was flecked with cold glitter. I was pricked open like a sieve.

He moved faster and faster on top of me, over me, inside me, and then there it was: he was bursting through me, and I was bursting through myself, and I thought that probably no two people had ever been more together, except for the tiny fact that one of them wasn't there at all.

MARK

The other day, I watched a movie about an island in Spain that wasn't really an island. It was a large piece of land floating on the surface of the Mediterranean, untethered to the seafloor. Its inhabitants went about their business as anybody would, fishing and cooking and sunning themselves on the beaches—but once in a while, a swell of current would rock the land from side to side, making them seasick. The film showed a diver exploring the island's underside: a shelf of scaly rock, covered with algae and moss. It was like some kind of submerged lunar surface. Like the sea had swallowed the moon.

It was this image that snagged my attention as I was flipping through the channels before bed as a way of turning off my brain. Reality show, reality show, *Everybody Loves Raymond* rerun, infomercial, reality show— then suddenly this otherworldly underwater landscape. At first I thought I'd imagined it—as though somehow my subconscious had projected it into my visual field. That was how deep, how private, the image felt. I put the remote down and watched the film all the way through to the end.

When I finally turned it off and made my way to the

bedroom, my girlfriend was lying on her half of the bed, turned toward the wall, pretending to sleep. I can always tell when she's pretending, and she only pretends when she's mad at me. After some coaxing, I learned why: apparently at one point she'd appeared in the doorway of the living room in her pajamas and asked me if I was coming to bed. I hadn't responded; I hadn't even looked in her direction, though she'd repeated her question two, then three times.

"Sometimes you frighten me," she said. "You just... check out. It's like nobody's home, like you've gone somewhere else."

I told her the truth—that I'd just been really interested in the movie—but this sounded dumb, even to me. I tried to explain that it hadn't really been about the film itself. But what it *was* about, I couldn't say; I only knew that those images had touched something in me and grazed it awake—some private, dark-tendriled thing I'd been trying to ignore.

After my girlfriend finally fell asleep—after I'd followed my feeble explanations with warm affirmations and tender, reassuring lovemaking—I lay awake thinking. Or not so much thinking as allowing the dark-tendriled thing to wave its fronds through my memory and brush old images to the surface. Images from those few months I lived with Zoe, when I got weirdly entangled—or re-entangled—with Rachel.

That time had been like suddenly finding yourself on

the underside of the island, realizing that it had never been an island in the first place. All along you'd thought you were on solid ground, but really you were floating. Once you knew of this underside's existence, it exerted a certain claim on you: sometimes you got sucked through to the other side, inaccessible to the sunny surface.

My girlfriend had been correct: I *had* disappeared for a moment. But I couldn't tell her where I'd gone, because still, even after all this time, I didn't know myself.

I never thought I would run into Rachel Starr again, not in real life. Certain people belong so completely to a particular time and place that they stay preserved in your mind there, as though trapped in a snow globe—you can nostalgically pick it up every now and then, give it a shake, feel something stir to the surface, but the scenes themselves don't change.

Of course she had been living some kind of adult life since I'd seen her last, at the end of our sophomore year of college. I'd even looked her up once or twice, curious whether she was on social media (she wasn't, which didn't surprise me; she'd always seemed impervious to that kind of thing). That's probably part of the reason I didn't really notice her, at first, when I saw her there behind the circulation desk at the Greenpoint library.

But I suppose it makes sense to start a bit earlier, to tell you how I ended up in Greenpoint in the first place— on my own for the first time in years, loose and adrift, a walking ellipsis, fatally vulnerable to magic.

I first heard about Zoe through Dan, a co-worker at the zoo. Dan was our Snake Guy. "My cousin has a room open at her place in Greenpoint," he'd said when I'd announced I was looking for a new apartment. "She's a little"—he twirled a finger around his ear—"but not in a bad way."

"What way are you defining as 'bad'?" I'd asked. To even become a Snake Guy, you need a pretty high threshold for craziness.

He thought about this for a minute. "The reality TV way, I guess. I mean she won't steal your shit or anything."

"So what's *good* crazy?"

"Fun crazy. Hippie crazy. You know—like, Burning Man."

"Oh. So she's into 'nature'?" I made air quotes. "She's high all the time?"

"No, I'm not sure she even *gets* high. She's one of those people that sort of seems high when she isn't."

"Hmm."

"I mean, like, she's always reading tarot cards or making a sculpture out of bird bones or something. She's pretty fun. She throws great parties."

I thought she sounded exhausting. Still, I was desperate. "I don't know, man," I said. "I've been going through a rough time, and—"

"Look, Zoe's cool with month by month, so why don't you just crash there till you find something better? It's only six hundred. You can save up. And she has a backyard."

I couldn't argue with this. Ana and I were still sharing the dingy junior one-bedroom in Murray Hill, the place where we'd come undone. It's hard to get over your ex-fiancée when you're still sleeping on the trundle bed beneath her, and every time she sneezes your mattress shakes.

The room in Zoe's apartment had peeling walls, yellow water stains on the ceiling, and a distinct smell (dank, salty, vaguely vaginal). But it also came with a free full-sized bed and a circular stained-glass window, now beaming a rose-shaped pattern of red and yellow light onto the opposite wall.

"Do you believe in prophecies?" she asked, looking up at me.

"Not really," I said.

"Well, I do," she said. "And you're going to live here."

"Oh yeah?"

"Yes," she said. "The cards told me so." She blinked her long lashes and smiled. She wasn't what I'd call *beautiful*, not exactly, not in the narrowest sense of the word—but she had these big googly blue-green eyes the color of peacocks. You know in cartoons when a character gets hit on the head and their eyes turn into revolving spirals? Her eyes had that effect. They kind of gave you vertigo. You had to look away first.

The ancient floorboards creaked beneath me as I walked into the room. You could *hear* a floorboard creak here. That's how quiet it was. The shouts and sirens of Manhattan felt oceans away.

I peeked into the small, cramped closet. "Not much in the way of storage, huh?" I said.

"Do you have a lot of stuff?"

"No. I guess I don't. My ex is keeping most of it."

I turned around. Zoe stood directly in front of the stained-glass window. Red and yellow light fell across her pale skin, her blond hair, her white dress. She looked like a woman-shaped column of flame.

She grinned. "So," she announced. "You love it."

I didn't, not exactly. But spoken aloud, her sentence seemed true, or as if it could be true—and how sweet, that declarative ring.

I believe in free will, not in fate. But will doesn't operate in a vacuum. Sometimes other people's are stronger than yours, and your will has no grounds for resistance. A feeling very much like fate enters your body and weakens it like a muscle relaxer; just like that, you find yourself living with a stranger in Brooklyn.

At least, that's how I see it now. At the time, I thought

I was simply making a rational decision. I granted Zoe
the faintly amused tolerance allowed to the temporary. I
could already imagine myself, years later, laughing while
I told the story about that time, *just* before my real life
started, when I lived in a tiny room in Greenpoint with a
girl who believed in prophecies.

And so, on the first day of August, I left Ana and Murray Hill with only two suitcases, a guitar I could barely play, and a feeling of tentative optimism about my prospects for emerging from a bewildering years-long funk. Bewildering because, when you graduate magna cum laude from Brown and move to New York with a girl you know you're going to marry, when the two of you snag twin research assistantships at twin elite hospitals, when you jointly purchase a couch and a blender and an engagement ring—when this is your life, a buoyant complacency sets in, easy to confuse with confidence. Your life stretches out before you like the colorful squares of a board game. You can hardly wait to pass go.

But this complacency is also a malaise, invisible until it's too late. Like some terrible STD. You glide smoothly down that line of colored squares until you find yourself sitting in front of a blank computer screen to write your med school personal statement, and realize you have nothing to say. "Describe your interest in the medical field." You can't think of a single thing. You write a few bullshitty paragraphs about your desire to help people. You mention your fascination with polymers, your extremely rewarding internship at NYU Langone. Your words stare back at you dumbly. Their patterns seem clumsy and meaningless, like trails left by a clod of dirt thrown at a wall.

It didn't help that Ana's personal statement seemed so effortless: she just sat down at the computer and this narrative unspooled onto the page in beautiful lucid prose—striking the perfect balance between ambition and humility, tough-mindedness and compassion, Mother Teresa and Jonas Salk. Everything that had ever happened to her since birth had led her directly to this moment, to the blinking cursor on her medical school application. Her essay vibrated with the force of this truth.

She didn't understand my sudden muteness. For the first time ever, static crackled between us. She tried to give me pep talks. She spoke of my "lack of confidence." But this was something bigger, something worse. Maybe I didn't want to be a doctor after all. Maybe I wanted to be a high school science teacher? A public intellectual? I could host a radio show about biology! A veterinarian? I had always been good with animals.

"You're grasping at straws," she finally said. "Look, maybe you just need some time off. The application grind is getting to you. Why not take a gap year? Do something different, something fun?"

And so the zoo became my gap year, and the gap became two years, then three. Slowly my life became one big gap. It yawned wider and wider every day. Ana stood on the edge of it, peering in, throwing rocks down and waiting for their thud to tell her how far away the bottom was. After a while there was no more bottom. I was entirely Gap.

I was aware that her indulgence of me carried an increasingly sharp whiff of contempt. Her Colombian immigrant parents would never have tolerated this wishy-washy *Who am I?* crap. "You pick a job and you *do* it," she said to me once. "That's what adulthood *is*." I knew that she was right. I deserved no sympathy for my malaise. My vacillations were a symptom of privilege. But wasn't that the *point* of having privilege, that you got to decide what to do with your life? Wasn't this why people like her parents, and my great-grandpa Art who came from Russia and worked his way up from shoeshine boy to head of the blah blah blah, worked so hard—so that their grandchildren had the privilege to take time and discern their own desires?

Yet my desires didn't become any clearer. Ana and I had nothing in common anymore. "Today I learned a cool fact about lemurs." "Today I delivered a baby." We stopped having sex. Once in a while she'd administer a brief, capable hand job. When I tried to slide a hand between her legs, she pulled it away.

No rancor, no screaming, just slow corrosion and grudging acceptance. In the end we sold her engagement ring on eBay, used the money to cover some of the extra rent and my moving costs. I had a feeling she'd be engaged again, to someone else, within a couple of years. (I was right.)

Two weeks after I moved in, I awoke to find Zoe next to me in bed, propped up on an elbow. She was watching me, as if she'd been waiting for me to wake up.

"I've been waiting for you to wake up," she said. She wore only an oversized John Lennon T-shirt that said IMAGINE.

"What's going on?" I mumbled, rubbing my eyes.

"I've got something to show you," she said. "But you have to promise first."

"Promise what?" I yawned, looking over at the clock: 6:30 a.m.

"A vow of silence," she said. "From the moment we leave your bed, we don't speak. That means the whole rest of the day. If you want to communicate, use gesture or write me a note."

"Why?"

"Something profound just happened in our backyard."

"What happened in our backyard?"

She shook her head, as if it were beyond explanation. "This is the last thing I'm going to say: I believe in the power of witnessing, untainted by verbal intervention. Are you with me or not?"

I shrugged. "Fine. If you don't want to talk, we won't talk."

She solemnly drew a finger across her lips. Then she

zipped mine too, leaving her finger a little longer than she needed to—in order, I guess, to communicate the gravity of the ritual. Then she took my hand, pulled me out of bed, and led me outside. I was still half asleep, and her finger's impression lingered on my lips.

It turned out a bat had visited our stamp-sized backyard the night before, given birth, and left the babies for dead. Little black-winged corpses lay strewn across the grass.

Zoe led me through the yard, pointing so I could watch my step. When we reached the back fence, she released my hand. I followed her gaze, and saw one little infant bat—the lone survivor—attempting to climb up the wooden fence post.

Something seized me, a feeling within striking range of awe: this raw newborn thing, struggling clumsily toward life. At the same time, I couldn't help but feel repulsed by this slick inch of dark winged muscle, its creepy humanoid fingers clutching at the metal, its delicate shoulder blades straining with effort, its muscles quivering beneath hairless translucent black skin. I thought: *demon fetus.*

I looked over at Zoe, but she didn't acknowledge me. Without taking her eyes from the bat, she slowly lifted the John Lennon T-shirt over her head and let it fall to the ground beside her. She wore no bra or underwear. The morning sunlight spilled over her breasts. I caught a glimpse of the shadowed region between her legs. Her long blond hair fell over her bare shoulders.

I knew that her gesture didn't necessarily have any-thing to do with sex: she'd told me how she'd once been kicked out of the MoMA for taking off her shirt in front of a painting, claiming in defense that it had "really touched" her "core," that she "just wanted to get closer to the art." (The guards weren't impressed.) Still, I felt that this performance in front of the bat had somehow been for my benefit. And I couldn't deny that, on some level, it was working.

Without a word I turned around, went inside, and took a cold shower. A few minutes later, toweling myself dry, I lifted a corner of the bathroom window blinds and saw her still standing there, naked, the sun on her shoulders, communing with the baby bat. Or whatever.

Like most people, I distrusted loose animals. I had a healthy respect for wildness and tried to grant it distance. Especially in the city: I knew that New York seethed subterraneously with teeth and fur, with rats and cock-roaches and squirrels and—who knew?—bats. But as far as those were concerned, I believed in a good-fences-good-neighbors policy. They could have the alleys and subway tunnels if I could have my few hundred square feet of human dwelling. If they infringed on this policy, I'd squash them.

But at the zoo it was another story.

During the summer we ran a special program for kids, a kind of animal camp. That day was Bug Day, which meant that after lunch we brought out a Madagascar hissing cockroach for the kids to touch. I felt no fear or disgust toward this cockroach. I was even fond of him. We'd named him Gregor Samsa, and sometimes it was easy to imagine him as a transformed Czech bank clerk. He had a very humanlike air of resignation. He submitted to routine indignities with something like, well, dignity.

We had this routine where he crawled up my arm and disappeared behind my neck while I narrated Fun Facts about his species. While he rounded the corner of my shoulder, I thought of Zoe and the bats, "untainted by verbal intervention," and I imagined her slinking in here at night and setting all our bugs free to rediscover their dark untame roots. She'd hinted at such desires when I told her what I did for a living. I imagined Gregor, born in a cage, trundling out into the wilds of the city, clueless and vulnerable as Kafka himself. I felt a kinship with him then, a vibration of sympathy. He obediently rounded my other shoulder; the children broke into wild applause.

When I got home from work, I found Zoe feeding the baby bat milk from an eyedropper. It was inside something like a terrarium, or empty fish tank lined with dirt and rocks. It clung to one of the glass walls, opening its mouth while Zoe squeezed a drop from above. She was back in the John Lennon T-shirt.

"You have got to be kidding me," I said.

She looked up and raised a finger to her lips.

"Fuck the vow of silence," I said. "That thing's going to give you rabies."

She finished squeezing out the drops of milk, giving no indication that she'd heard me. Then she looked up, raised one finger in a wait-a-minute gesture, stood, and carried the terrarium outside. When she came back in, she went straight to the sink and washed her hands vigorously, up to the elbow, using tons of soap, looking back over her shoulder to make sure I was watching her.

Finally, she shook her hands off, flinging arcs of water droplets through the kitchen. They caught the sunlight as they passed in front of the window, so it looked as though she was shaking off little beads of light. Then she walked over to me, put one finger over my lips, and put her other hand down my pants.

Dan was right: Zoe threw good parties.

Drunk on some kind of herb-infused liquor, I let a girl named Raven read my aura. It was green.

There were multiple Hula-Hoopers. There was a woman painting flowers and third eyes on people's faces. There were many indeterminately gendered people making out with each other. I counted three women dressed as mermaids. A guy with a handlebar mustache walked around on stilts. Several women and one man wiggled their butts against me and laughed. One of them called me "Daddy." At one point I found myself at the bottom of a human pyramid. Toward the end of the night—

the beginning of the morning—a man who introduced himself as Dr. Volcano literally breathed fire.

When the party finally started to dwindle, I noticed that Zoe was missing. I went back into the house to look for her and found her on the couch, half naked, intertwined with another woman. I think it was the aura reader, Raven.

One month went by, then two, and I didn't look for another apartment. In other respects I was clawing my way back to productive adulthood: I spent my weekends at the coffee shop with my laptop, researching various graduate programs in environmental science and studying for the GREs. I emailed my college professors and internship supervisors to ask for recommendations. I even began a few tentative flirtations with women in the neighborhood. But I found myself unable, or unwilling, to wrestle my way out of Zoe's sexual orbit.

Sleeping with her was like sleeping with a thunderstorm. She had some kind of weird sexual intuition that enabled her to know what I wanted before I knew it myself. She also had a certain attentiveness to detail, a mastery of nuance. (I hadn't realized that when you touched *that* place on my whatever while doing a little twisty motion to *that* part of my whatever whatever, it would result in, well...*that*.) I still thought of this period as temporary, an aberration—but now, I could also see it as educational.

Still, the drawbacks of the situation were obvious. A couple of times, I tried to bring home other women.

Both times, Zoe was unavoidable: sitting on the couch in just her underwear, flipping through a magazine, her long blond hair only partially obscuring her nipples, or burning incense while working on a sculpture in the kitchen—saturating the apartment with her sexual dominance.

Once, I awoke with a woman I'd met at a bar the night before to find that Zoe had made breakfast for the three of us; she set out pancakes, berries, honey, and a pot of coffee and then joined us at the table, stark naked except for a moth-eaten white slip that hid absolutely nothing—that somehow seemed more obscene than nudity itself. She kept touching my arm and asking me to pass the honey, letting her hand linger just a little too long each time. The woman slunk away the first chance she got.

When Zoe rotated in a lover from her well-stocked stable, however, I always seemed to conveniently take up as little space as possible. I'd be at my computer with my big noise-canceling headphones on, and I wouldn't even notice them come in; when I took off the headphones to pee, I'd hear Zoe's giggles and moans. Or I'd bump into the person awkwardly on my way to the bathroom. Or I'd come in to find them making out on the couch, and have to scuttle past them like a crab.

On nights when she didn't have anyone, Zoe would often—but never predictably—sidle up to me on the couch and slide her hand down my pants. Just like that. No prelude: one moment she wasn't there, the next she was touching my penis. It was lightning war, sexual blitzkrieg. The mornings after she passed through my room—inhabiting my bed like a bright booming darkness, leaving me loose and empty and not quite sated—a distinct tinge of despair crept into my postcoital haze. I wasn't in love with this woman, I wasn't even sure that I *liked* her, and yet, as long as I lived here, we were bound, electron to atom. I couldn't tell if I was over Ana or not. I couldn't tell if I was happy. I just lived from moment to moment, evening to evening, in strict sexual survival mode.

Finally, as the two-month mark passed—as we entered October, and skulls and fake spiderwebs bloomed across the facades of rickety Greenpoint houses—I began to think seriously about leaving. But my first few preliminary scans of Craigslist showed that rents had gone up in just the few months since my last search: to live in any desirable neighborhood in Manhattan or Brooklyn, I'd have to pay double or even triple what I was paying Zoe. Even Queens was barely within my grasp. Though technically that borough wasn't far away, and although it was traversed by all the same train lines I used every day, I didn't know anyone who lived there; signing a one-year lease out in Astoria or Jackson Heights seemed like Napoleonic exile. Still, I looked at some listings, sent a few exploratory emails.

Then, though—then I ran into Rachel, and everything changed.

What happened was, I ran out of free online GRE practice tests, so I went to the library to get more. Lately I'd become addicted to practice tests. Studying made me feel, despite Zoe's siren calls, as though I was finally getting somewhere, as though my ship was sailing in the right direction. Lately I'd been spending long stretches of time away from the apartment, tearing my way through analogies and algebra problems. It was my way of strapping myself to the mast, plugging my ears, moving forward.

At first I only noticed her, there behind the library desk, in a nonspecific way—in that dark region of the brain that exists specifically for noticing cute girls, that faintly hums whenever one comes into its range. Semiconsciously I registered her pretty heart-shaped face, her dark bob, her thick black-framed glasses, her red lipstick.

And then a shudder of recognition kicked in: this wasn't just any cute girl. It was *her*.

My infatuation with Rachel Starr had consumed more than half of my college career. It started in a creative writing class freshman year. Rachel was the quiet girl on the other side of the seminar table who almost never spoke in class but turned in these brief, brilliant, odd pieces of writing: nuggets of dialogue that seemed as though they'd been translated from a different language, perhaps a language spoken by aliens or fish; strange little fables set in alternate universes; eerie portraits of cracked domesticity that made you feel as though you'd never *really* seen certain objects before (a spatula, a crocheted tissue box cover, the gelatinous web of light cast by a fish tank in a dark room).

I'd signed up for the class on a whim, faintly enjoying the idea of reinventing myself as a Writer, or at least as Someone Who Wrote. Unfortunately, I was terrible. I had no imagination. I could only research and mimic. It was exhausting: when you really thought about words, there was far too much to think about. How might a good writer describe a human nose, for example? What kind of noses were there, besides "Roman" and "aquiline"? What did those words even mean? This was how I spent my writing time: looking up words like "aquiline" in the dictionary, and then tortuously composing some labored scene of domestic strife between an unhappy housewife and her aquiline-nosed husband. I was miserable, certain I was fooling no one.

Then, one week, the teacher sorted us into "buddies," to exchange rough drafts and discuss our writing processes outside of class, and Rachel was paired with me. Surprisingly, she seemed genuinely interested in my stories: I could do the one thing she couldn't (stick to a linear narrative). She didn't write the way she did on purpose, she confessed. She just didn't know how else to do it. She wrote what came into her head, what pleased her, but these fits of inspiration never lasted longer than a page or two. How, she wanted to know, did a plausible narrative accrue, page after page? I shrugged and said something like "I guess I just think about what the character would be likely to do next." She nodded, eyes wide, as though this had never occurred to her.

I don't think it took her long to see through me. But by that point we were "involved." At the end of that very first meeting, I invited her to see a movie downtown. She hesitated, bit her lip, then said yes. After that it was she who took the initiative: she who kissed me at the end of the night, who waited after the next class meeting for me to walk her home. Soon we were spending hours at a time conducting vigorous sexual experiments in our lumpy dorm room beds.

There was a lot to discover. We'd both already lost our virginities, but only in the most technical of senses. Sometimes I got the feeling there was something imper-sonal and scientific about our sex: that she was using me as a kind of experiment, to game out her body's various possibilities. It didn't matter. I was smitten. The fact of her body, of my access to it, stunned me. I never got used to it.

Over time we became a real couple, at least on the surface: we slept together several nights a week, spent breaks with each other's families, talked about getting an off-campus apartment together our junior year. But I always had the sneaking suspicion that we weren't *really* together. Sometimes it seemed as though these pretenses at couplehood were just her way of humoring me while she worked toward some other, mysterious end.

Each step we took in our relationship was proposed by me: calling each other boyfriend and girlfriend, meeting each other's parents, possibly moving in together. She never objected, but she never initiated either. When I said "I love you," she dutifully repeated it back, but she never said it first. I came to suspect that she was approaching the relationship as a whole with the same attitude she had toward sex: a detached, clinical curiosity about what might happen next. I, on the other hand, grew only more obsessed, dependent upon whatever it was she gave me—or perhaps upon what she withheld.

Sometimes I'd catch her staring into space, clearly elsewhere, but when I asked her what she was thinking about, she'd flinch, as if snapping awake, and then say "What?" as if she wasn't aware she'd been gone. As her strange stories suggested, she viewed the world at a slant—as though she'd come from some entirely different realm, a curious alien in a person suit. For me— a premed student who spent his days looking through a microscope at the granular, visible motions to which life could be reduced—her attunement to some invisible register was endlessly fascinating. The longer I knew her, the more I wanted to see what she saw, to go where she went.

So I was devastated, but not surprised, when she calmly informed me that she'd fucked her downstairs neighbor, and that she guessed that meant we had to break up.

"Are you in love with him?" I asked.

"No."

"Are you going to do it again?"

"Probably not."

"Is there anyone *else* you want to fuck?"

"No, not really."

"Then we don't have to break up—do we?"

She frowned; she seemed to not have considered this possibility—the possibility that I might forgive her, that we might be able to work things out. She didn't seem opposed to the idea, but when I tried to get her to explain the reason for her dissatisfaction, she couldn't. She mumbled something about "the daydream," but when I pressed her, she couldn't articulate what she meant.

I couldn't even bring myself to be mad at her. She seemed so genuinely confused, so baffled by her own motivations. It was only after she'd definitively broken up with me (still without an explanation), only after she'd stopped responding to my emails and calls, that I finally thought to myself, *That was kind of fucked up.*

For months, I talked to whoever would listen—my

friends, my mom, a counselor at student health services, random townies in Providence bars—about how unfair it all was. Hadn't I been a good boyfriend, an attentive lover? Hadn't she claimed to return my feelings? Did she even *have* feelings, or was she some kind of robot?

Finally, one day, my friend Omar said, "At this point, man, *you're* fucked up, and you can't even blame it on her. That statute of limitations has passed. You gotta shut *up* about this." I didn't listen to him right away—I spent that night on the floor in my dorm hallway because I was too drunk to fit the key into the lock—but when I woke up the next morning with a massive hangover, I realized he was right. I stopped contacting Rachel. I started going to the gym for several hours a day. I began flirting with my lab partner.

That lab partner turned out to be Ana, and Ana turned out to be, in a way, the reason I now found myself in this very library, where Rachel apparently worked— this library not five blocks from my new apartment, where normal people came in for normal reasons and interacted with her in normal ways, as if she herself was a normal person and not some apparition from the past, an incursion of some alternate reality into my tenuously ordered life.

I managed, somehow, to move. I walked to the back of the library, where I could calmly consider what to do. I watched Rachel from the corner of my eye while pretending to examine a row of books about Lyndon B. Johnson.

I probably could have walked out right then, undetected. But it felt suddenly important to not avoid the encounter, even—especially—if that meant humiliating myself. Wasn't this the lesson my life was trying to teach me? That I had to burn my old self up completely before something new might rise from the ashes?

I went over to the test prep section, picked up a few GRE books, and walked purposefully to the counter. And there she was, sitting right in front of me: those big brown eyes behind the thick glasses, those bright-red lips, those smooth cheeks. I'd cupped that face in my palm so many times. I could have reached out and done it now.

"Just a second," she said, eyes on her computer.

"Okay," I said.

She typed something into the computer screen, hit Enter, then looked up.

The series of reactions that broke over her face was so

legible it might as well have been subtitled. She met me with a distant professional gaze; then something snagged and caught. She frowned, her eyes widened—*Could it be?*—and finally her cheeks flushed bright red.

"Oh," she said. "*Oh.* Um...hi."

"Hi," I said. Her visible loss of composure was more gratifying than I could have hoped. Despite myself, I grinned.

"What—how are you? Do you live around here?" she stammered.

"I do," I said. "As of a few months ago. You?"

"I just work here," she said. "I live in Clinton Hill."

"Oh. Hmm."

I'd never known her to be so inarticulate. Her face had a tight, pained look, as though she was on the verge of tears. Somehow this emboldened me.

"Listen," I said, "it's so crazy to run into you here. Why don't we catch up sometime?"

"Well...okay."

"Want to grab a drink when you get off work?"

"You mean *today?*"

"Why not? Or some other day, if you're busy."

She shook her head. "I'm not busy."

"Okay then. When are you off?"

I was halfway home before I realized I'd forgotten the GRE books. Still, I felt triumphant. I'd encountered a person who'd once had the power to destroy me, and I'd remained calm. Whatever happened next, I'd already won.

Did that mean she had lost? She seemed to have lost *something:* she didn't seem as self-contained, as clearly defined, as before. Had she, too, been buffeted and blurred by life, eroded by adult ambiguities, in the half decade since we'd seen each other?

When I got to Manhattan Inn at six on the dot, Rachel was already there, sitting at the bar with a half-empty glass of white wine in front of her, her chin resting on her hand.

"You're early," I said.

She turned and gave a faint smile. "I slipped out before closing," she said. "I needed a drink."

"Rough day?" I settled myself on the stool next to hers.

She shrugged, as if to say, *No rougher than any other.*

I decided not to press. Instead, I ordered an IPA. Then I turned to her. "So," I said. "Fill me in. You're living in Clinton Hill, and you work at the library."

"Yeah. That's about it. I went to library school right out of undergrad, and I've been working there ever since."

"Library school. Hmm."

"Yeah. I realized I needed to touch books."

"To touch them?"

"I realized the world outside my head didn't feel completely real unless I could touch it. I like to *read* the books too, of course. But I didn't have the stamina to be a writer. Or an academic. You remember how I could never finish anything."

"I hope you still write, though? Even just for yourself?"

She shrugged. "Kind of." She traced a pattern with her finger on the surface of the bar, then looked up. "What about you? Are you, like, a doctor by now?"

"Well. Not exactly."

"'Not exactly' like not yet?"

"Like not at all. I kind of…changed paths. I'm working at the zoo now."

"The zoo? Like…taking care of giraffes?"

I laughed. "They have an education department. We teach kids about animals and the environment. It's something I sort of fell into."

"I bet you're good at that."

I shrugged. "I mean, I've been doing it for a while now. For years I debated whether it was a good use of my biology degree. On the one hand, it definitely wasn't; on the other, I liked it. So. Anyway, it was never supposed to be a forever thing. I'm applying to grad school now. Environmental science."

She nodded thoughtfully. "Doctors don't really get it, anyway," she said.

"Don't get what?"

She made a fluttery gesture, indicating the space around us. "You know. *It*. The substrate of everything."

I had no idea what she meant, but decided not to pursue it.

"So," she said. "Now you live here."

"Yeah."

"With…?" Her eyes flicked down to my ring-free

hand, then back up. "I guess I kind of figured you'd be married by now."

"No, not married." I hesitated for a second. How did I explain Zoe? "But I'm—yeah, I guess I'm living with a girl. It's complicated."

She nodded. "I'm in an it's-complicated too," she said.

I waited for her to say more, but she didn't. She just took another sip of her wine and looked down at her hands. She frowned, and I thought I saw that look come into her eyes, that distant gaze. I felt a familiar dumb panic: *Don't go.*

"I got engaged, actually," I blurted out. "To Ana."

"Oh," she said, looking up.

"But we broke up. About six months ago."

"I'm sorry."

"It's okay. It's better this way. It's just kind of... disorienting. I'm not even sure I miss *her,* specifically. It's more like... you don't realize, while it's happening, how much what a partner gives you is simply... context. Being on my own now is kind of like living in another country. Canada, maybe. Everything looks the same, and everybody understands the words I'm saying, and yet I feel kind of..."

"Adrift."

"Yes." I looked at her with surprise: she'd spoken eagerly, almost *too* eagerly, like a game show contestant ready with the correct answer. She stared at me now with an unfamiliar fixity, her eyes fastened on mine; she had the look of someone on the brink of a propulsive, unsolicited self-disclosure. I held my breath, trying not to startle the moment away.

But then she leaned back, took another sip of her wine, and sighed. "So," she said. "Who are you living with now? You were starting to say."

"Just this girl Zoe," I said. "She's sort of a friend of a friend. I moved into her house to get away from the situation with Ana. And now I'm—I don't know. She's kind of weird. It's a little bit unsustainable. But I keep staying, for some reason. I guess because—"

"Because you're fucking her?" she blurted, a mischievous glint in her eyes.

I paused, stunned.

She giggled. "You *are*," she said. "You're totally fucking her." Then she laughed again—a clear, hiccupy, infectious giggle—and I found myself laughing too.

Then the whole story tumbled out of me: the tarot cards, the baby bats, the blitzkrieg sex. Rachel thought all of it was hilarious. At one point—I think the point when I described the baby bat in the terrarium—she laughed so hard that she practically lost her breath: her face grew red, her inhalations choked and wheezy. She finally had to put her forehead on the bar and clutch her stomach in order to catch her breath.

When I finished the story, she shook her head from side to side and said, "Thank you. *Thank* you. That's the hardest I've laughed in a long time."

"Uh, happy to oblige." I didn't even care that my life was the butt of the joke. I watched with satisfaction as she wiped away the small tears that had gathered at the corners of her eyes, as she took a restorative sip of wine, as her breathing returned to normal and her laughter-blotched skin regained its even pallor.

"Okay," I said. "Your turn."

"For what?"

"I told you about my it's-complicated, now I wanna hear about yours."

Immediately I wished the sentence back into my mouth. She flinched, as if struck; then she sat straight up and furrowed her brow.

"Can I ask you something?" she said, her voice suddenly low and dead serious.

"Shoot."

"Do you think your roommate Zoe is...for real? I mean, I know she's kind of ridiculous, but do you think she knows what she's talking about? Like, can she really..."

"Can she really do what?"

"I don't know." She shrugged, looked down at her near-empty wineglass. "Like, it sounds dumb, but is she really some kind of witch or something?"

"I have no idea," I said. "I mean, I wouldn't know how to figure that out."

"Never mind. I just—I'm curious. Some weird stuff has been happening to me lately."

"What kind of weird stuff?"

"I can't really explain it. But—I don't know. Do you believe in spirits? Ghosts?"

"Ghosts like *Boo*?"

She shook her head. "I shouldn't have mentioned it. Sorry. Even the question sounds idiotic. I mean, you're a *scientist*."

"No, no. I didn't mean to trivialize…anything. Whatever it was you were gonna tell me."

She looked down at her wineglass. "Well," she said. "It's just—I know someone. Someone who died. And—"

"Oh, and you want to…communicate with them? Like, with a medium? That kind of thing?"

"No. Not exactly." She opened her mouth, then closed it again. "Never mind," she said. "It doesn't really make sense anyway." But she looked as she had when I'd first spoken to her in the library: tense, fragile, blurred. Her eyes started to glisten; she blinked, clearly holding back tears.

"Hey." I reached out and laid a hand on her arm. "Are you okay?"

She jerked away from me, sharply, as if my touch had scalded her. Then she leapt off the barstool and took a step away from me, shrinking into herself.

I opened my mouth to speak but was distracted by something: a sharp, tingly feeling had begun to play over my hand where it had come into contact with Rachel's skin, as if the air around my fingers was suddenly fizzing like seltzer.

She stared at her hand, then at me, then back at her arm. "I have to go," she whispered.

"Don't go, don't go," I said. I reached out to try and hold her in place, but she ducked away from my grip and began clumsily pulling on her jacket.

"This was wrong," she said. "I knew it was wrong."

"What was wrong?" My voice sounded embarrassingly high. "I didn't mean to scare you. I know you don't want..." The sentence trailed off; what I really meant was *You don't want me,* but I felt myself unable to speak the words, to make them true again.

She gave me a weary look. "You don't know anything," she said. Then, without looking back, she walked briskly to the door, pushed it open, and disappeared.

I sat there at the bar for a long time, doing nothing, thinking nothing—only picturing her face as she'd pulled away, remembering the strange tingly feeling that had played over my hand.

Finally I settled up and left. But I couldn't imagine going home. I started walking with no purpose other than momentum itself, crossing the street when I had the signal, turning the corner when I didn't. As I walked, Rachel's final words echoed through my mind. *You don't know anything. You don't know anything.*

I found myself crossing McCarren Park, heading toward the big Russian church at the park's southern edge. I'd noticed this church many times before; with its bulbous dome, its four onion-shaped spires, it was hard to miss. But I'd never taken a particular interest in it. Today, though, I found myself drawing closer, walking up the steps, gently pushing open the door and going inside. It seemed like a good place to sit and collect myself.

No one was there besides a thin bearded man rustling around up front, doing some fussy kind of maintenance: rearranging Bibles or something like that. I sat down in one of the back pews and looked around. The space was cavernous, dim but expansive, with lambent stained-glass windows and soaring domed ceilings. The kind of place that both amplifies and diminishes your sense of self. I felt the calculating, reptilian part of my brain retracting like a blade, making room for some downier, more diffuse sort of consciousness. I sat there for a few minutes, just looking around and spacing out, feeling my adrenaline dissipate into the thin slanted light.

Then something strange happened. A bell rang out, and as the sound hit my body, a dark emotion shot through me. I felt perforated, literally nauseous with sadness, as if I was going to be sick. I crumpled, leaning over and putting my head between my knees.

I had no idea where the feeling had come from, or to what it referred—only that it was connected somehow to the light through the windows and the sound of the bell and the sense memory of Rachel's touch. I felt as though I was going to cry, but I couldn't. I even tried squeezing my eyes to release tears, but nothing came out.

There was nothing I could do but shudder against the feeling, rocking myself slowly until it passed. I looked up. The church had grown dim. The man in front was still arranging Bibles; he'd moved a few pews back but seemed unaware of me. I got up and walked out into the cold darkening evening.

I took the long way home, weaving through the twilit streets of Greenpoint, absorbing the aftereffects of the inexplicable feeling that had seized me in the church, running over the entire day's events in my mind.

I might have thought I'd imagined it, the tingle on my hand where my skin had touched Rachel's, except that she seemed to have noticed it too. I remembered the startled look on her face, the way she'd looked from her hand to my own and then back again. *You don't know anything. You don't know anything.*

As I walked, the memory of that feeling combined with other memories—certain curves of her body, seen in the dim light of my dorm room seven years before. As I drew closer and closer to home, these musings called up a certain state of bodily alertness, of specific hunger.

When I got into the apartment and saw Zoe standing at the kitchen sink washing dishes, with her back to me—her blond hair cascading down her back, nearly grazing the waist of the booty shorts she wore as pajamas—I felt inspired to do something I hadn't done before: to initiate.

If Zoe had heard me come in, she didn't show it. Sometimes she acted like this, fake nonchalant, ignoring my presence. She probably knew that it thickened the erotic brew to make me wait.

Tonight, though, I couldn't. I came up behind her, pulled the pot out of her hand, turned off the faucet, then reached around and cupped her breasts. She gave a sharp intake of breath—from surprise or arousal or both, I wasn't sure. I left my hands on her breasts for a moment and then trailed one downward, sliding it between her legs. She didn't move.

I'd faintly expected some teasing comment, some gentle mockery of my libido, a light dismissive laugh—"What's gotten into you tonight, tiger?" But she didn't say anything. She just waited, calm yet tense, her body alerted to mine the way two animals become alert when they stun each other in a clearing. For the first time, she awaited my move. I did too. I honestly didn't know what I'd do next. I only knew that for now I had to stand here, to wait, to make her wait.

Ever so slowly, I increased the pressure. She grew slick beneath my hand, and her breathing quickened. But still I didn't move.

Finally Zoe whispered something, so softly I almost couldn't make it out:

"Tell me her name."

"What?"

"Tell me her name," she said again, louder.

I turned her around and kissed her roughly on the mouth.

That night, I had a strange dream. I almost never dream—or at least remember dreaming—so this fact was unsettling in and of itself. In the dream, I woke up in bed, but it was Rachel next to me, rather than Zoe. She was curled up on her side, facing away from me, the way she always used to sleep. Her hair was splayed out on the pillow behind her, leaving the downy skin of her neck exposed; her body faintly glowed in the moonlight pouring through the stained-glass window.

I reached out to touch her. But as soon as my hand made contact with her skin, she dissolved into a quivering black mass that then exploded into a cloud of baby bats.

The little black-winged creatures started flying around the room, shrieking like crows. Somehow, this was both terrifying and arousing. As they flew, my body started to tingle all over—the way my hand had tingled when I'd touched Rachel's arm earlier that day. My arousal was connected directly to the bats' flight patterns; it was as if they were attached to me by invisible energetic cords, and so the chaotic zigzags and circles they made in the air pulled something toward the surface of my body, just below the skin—something quivering and mobile, that wanted to escape into the room's swirl of bodies. If this happened, I knew, I would die—the flesh container called Mark Samuels would cease to exist. And yet this burst of entropic flight was what my body wanted. The dark pulse inside me, the tingle on the surface of my skin—they wanted to meet, to turn me inside out.

Suddenly, one of the bats drew closer, hovering in place just a few inches from my face. His eyes were dark beads, his skin shadowy and translucent, his muscles straining and clutching to keep his wings in motion. The bat regarded me with a frank, humanlike gaze; then he opened his mouth and spoke.

"Desire never dies," said the bat. "It only changes form." Then he flew into my mouth.

The sound of my own voice woke me up: I was yelling, trying to expel the baby bat from my throat. I could *feel* his body in there: the rough mammalian squirm against my throat's slick walls, the pinching movements of his wings as he tried to force himself inside me.

I stopped yelling, raised my hands to my throat. I swallowed a couple of times, to prove that I could. I was soaked in sweat, and my heart was still pounding. I could still hear the bats' shrieks, see the blur of their bodies, feel the vibration of their wingbeats trembling through the air. I could still feel the tingle on the surface of my skin and the dark roiling beneath. *Desire never dies.*

Had it *all* been a dream? The sex I'd initiated with Zoe?

My meeting with Rachel? No—there was Zoe's underwear on the floor where I'd pulled it off last night. There were her shorts hanging over the edge of the bed frame. And when I closed my eyes, I could see Rachel's face so clearly. I could still feel that fizzy aftereffect of our touch. I could see her walking away. *You don't know anything.*

I didn't go back to the library. Actually, I did pass the building once, a few days later. But I couldn't bring myself to go inside. Approaching the building, I saw Rachel through the window, and stopped in my tracks. It was already dark outside, and the inside was lit up with a yellow glow, like a stage. She sat there in profile, hands folded on her desk, frowning as if thinking very hard about something.

Everything about her posture—the spine so straight it could have been pulled from above on invisible wire, the light way her hands rested on the table, her ankles delicately crossed beneath her chair—suggested a person trying very hard to hold herself together. There was a tension to her, like the tension of a ballerina or acrobat, someone who constantly battled invisible downward-pulling forces. I didn't understand her—I never had—but I *felt* her. It made my heart ache. I turned around and walked home.

That night, sitting across the table from Zoe as we shared takeout Indian, I said, "Can I ask you something?"

"Shoot."

"Do you consider yourself a...witch? Or...I don't know the proper term. I don't know what you 'identify' as." I made air quotes.

She laughed. "What do you mean?"

I shook my head. "I don't know. I just—I don't understand it, a lot of the stuff you do. Like, can you...talk to spirits? Or anything like that?"

She leaned back in her chair and regarded me coolly, with a faintly amused smile. "I thought you didn't believe in that stuff," she said.

"I don't," I said. "Or, well—I mean, personally, I have no reason to. I'm agnostic. I'm sort of...asking for a friend."

"Which friend?"

"To be honest, she's my ex. I just ran into her in the neighborhood. She works at the library, I guess. We ended up getting a drink, and I mentioned that you had some background in occult stuff or whatever, and she seemed interested. I guess she knows someone who died recently, and that's why."

She raised an eyebrow. "Your ex, huh?"

"Not my ex-fiancée. This is my ex-girlfriend from college. Rachel."

"Rachel. *Rachel.*" She repeated the name to herself, as if testing out how it sounded. Then she nodded. "So you met Rachel, you got a drink, and she asked you if you knew any psychics?"

"Well, not exactly. I mean, it didn't exactly happen like that."

She laughed. "Of course not." She shook her head from side to side, a gesture that I'd come to read as *You're hopeless.* "Let me guess: you guys were just catching up, talking about relationships and stuff, and all of a sudden she mentioned her dead friend and got all vulnerable and wounded."

I didn't say anything, but my face must have given me away.

Zoe laughed. "You're so cute, Mark," she said. "You really had no idea what she was doing?"

"She was *doing* something?"

This, apparently, was the funniest thing Zoe had ever heard. She laughed even harder, doubling over and hooting, then finally murmuring "Oh my God, oh my God" while slowing her breath, just as she did after an orgasm.

Often, in the moments when we weren't actively having sex, I got the feeling that I was the butt of some private joke for Zoe, that she enjoyed a constant low-level amusement at my relative prudery. But she'd never actually *laughed* at me before, not out loud.

"Are we done here?" I said.

"Listen," she said, still catching her breath. "Listen, let me explain something to you. Girls like this? I mean, girls who act all helpless around their ex-boyfriends who are clearly still in love with them and ask for recommendations for a *psychic*—"

"But I'm not—she wasn't—"

"Shh. Just lean back and appreciate it for a second."

"Appreciate what?"

"How expertly she's seduced you." She shrugged. "But anyway, sure, I'll play along. If she wants to come talk to me about her dead friend, I'm game. Or I'm happy to give you an excuse to bring her over. Sounds interesting."

"You think that's what I'm really asking you to do? To help me get my ex into bed? Give me a little credit, Zoe."

"But I bet that's what you really want."

"Well—" I felt my face turn red.

"I knew it," she said. She slapped the surface of the table and giggled. "Markie has a girrrrrlfriend!"

"God, Zoe, what are we, in sixth grade?"

"I'm just having fun."

"What about you?" I said.

"What *about* me?"

"What's *your* game?"

"What do you mean?"

"Why do you want to help me hook up with Rachel? So that once I've brought her here you can scare her away?"

"I don't know what you're talking about," she said. She smiled sweetly. "I don't scare anybody."

"Never mind," I said. "Why bother? Look, I'm going to bed."

She shrugged. "Fine. But if you want, Markie, I'll be your wingwoman. I won't fuck anything up for you. Scout's honor." She sat up straight and held two fingers up in the Scout's pledge position, then separated them into a V and thrust her tongue between them. I rolled my eyes, and she collapsed into giggles.

"Forget about it," I said. "This whole thing is too weird."

"What thing?"

"This," I said. "Everything. You. Rachel. Brooklyn. All of it."

"Listen," she said, getting up. She pulled her bag off the back of her chair, extracted her wallet, and rummaged around for something. "Ah. Yes. Here it is." She held out a business card. "Take it."

The card read,

DR. B MOON

METAPHYSICAL ACUPUNCTURE

Underneath was an address on Thirty-Second Street.

"Metaphysical acupuncture?" I asked.

Zoe shrugged. "Dr. Moon is kind of my guru," she said. "You can pass this on to your friend if you want. And then she can ask me about it when she comes over."

"*If* she comes over."

"Right. If." She winked.

"Anyway, uh, thanks, I guess. Good night."

"Night," she said with a languid shrug. She plopped back into the chair, took another sip of her tea.

But when I paused by my bedroom door and turned back to look at her, her arms were folded and she was staring into space, her brow furrowed. I had never seen Zoe look like this—look *worried*—before.

I wasn't yet sure what to do about Rachel—whether or not I should try to see her again. But one thing was certain: in the week that followed, she became an invisible yet palpable presence in my shared life with Zoe, hovering constantly at its edges. We never mentioned her again, but something was different. Our interactions took on that charge that can only come from triangulation, from the loom of an outside presence. We were always aware of Rachel—the way that you might live a mile inland and still faintly smell the ocean, taste its salt beneath your covers, or on your skin.

The balance of power had shifted. I no longer waited dumbly on the couch for Zoe's periodic assaults. Now, instead, we did nothing for long stretches of time—orbiting each other, skirting the charged field that lay between us—and then, when the tension threatened to boil over, one of us would attack. She would come up behind me and leap onto my back, attaching her mouth to my neck like a jackal or a vampire, or I would step into the shower after her and yank her wet rope of hair into my fist.

* * *

Meanwhile, I managed to stick to my schedule—to continue going through the motions at work, to prep for the GRE—but I couldn't shake my restlessness. Even the genial puppet show I'd always done for the younger kids at the zoo took a dark turn. Edgar the Elephant (played by me), a talk show host who interviewed various members of the animal kingdom, started to go off script: sassing his guests ("So how's it feel to be the third-fastest runner in the animal kingdom? I mean, that's what every athlete hopes for, right? A bronze medal?") or interrupting them to tickle them or insult their morphological traits ("So, Lizzie, I hear you have a cloaca. What's that like?"). Sometimes he didn't ask any questions at all, just went off on ranty monologues about ivory poachers. My colleagues, playing Edgar's guests, gamely attempted responses to his increasingly off-kilter presence, often struggling through their own laughter. The show got less and less educational each time, but the more inappropriate Edgar became, the more the kids loved him, so nobody gave me a problem about it. I was practically the most senior person in the department by then anyway.

To make matters worse, it seemed as though that month all the zoo animals were doing it, everywhere and all the time, conspicuously.

I became more aware than ever of the ridiculous equipment Mother Nature had bestowed on her creations for the purpose of fucking. Not only the flamboyant signals of sexual availability—the peacocks with their impractical plumage—but the plumbing itself. The tapir had a penis nearly the length of his body; sometimes, when it was semiflaccid, he stepped on it by accident while padding around his pen. This didn't seem to bother him. Odd, how a penis could sometimes be a barely noticed encumbrance, and other times could become the captain of one's existence.

The classroom where we conducted our educational activities at the zoo bordered the silverback pen, or "habitat," as we euphemistically called it, separated only by a giant floor-to-ceiling window. When this window was uncovered, we could look directly in on the gorilla family: Bud; Marie; their babies, Stella and Josephine; and a few aunts and uncles.

It was a wonderful moment, usually right after we'd distributed the kids' afternoon snacks on the first day of a program, when someone slowly drew back the curtain for the first time. The children would gasp, then abandon their carrot sticks and flock to the window, suddenly face-to-face with a family of gorillas. They pressed their little hands and noses up against the glass, and Bud and company hammed it up in return: wrestling, doing somersaults, occasionally even coming up to the window and pressing their hands to the children's, prison visit–style. To anyone watching, it was eerily obvious how close our species actually were: the children's faces were suddenly the faces of primates, the gorillas' eyes undeniably protohuman. You had the profound sense that they knew us, perhaps as well as we knew them. Or better.

But one day that week, a kid shrieked, dropped his juice box, and yelled, "What are they *doing*?!"

You can guess what they were doing. We had to run over and close the curtain, as quickly as we could, while putting on a DVD of *The Lorax* to distract the kids, pretending that this had somehow been the plan all along.

It seemed kind of stupid, our frantic effort to conceal this part of nature from our nature curriculum, but I could imagine the kind of phone calls we'd get from concerned parents otherwise—parents who wanted to keep their children in some sort of preoedipal Eden despite the fact that they lived in the world's most libidinous city, where no one could stay innocent for long.

It happened with Rachel, in the end, like everything else that happened after I moved to Brooklyn: inexplicably, independently of my conscious will, seemingly by magic.

It had been a particularly exhausting day. I'd done a snake demo, explained the difference between reptiles and amphibians at least four times, helped a kid out of his urine-soaked clothes after he got overexcited at the prairie dog exhibit, wiped multiple snotty noses. I'd performed Edgar the Elephant twice, and both times I got the sense that I was actually beginning to make people uneasy: when I came out from behind the puppet theater, most kids were still laughing, but several wore the distinct look of holding back tears.

At the end of the day, after our staff meeting, my boss, Cathy Horn, pulled me aside. "Can I talk to you?" she asked.

"Sure. What's up?"

"I mean in my office."

Cathy Horn—who none of us could bring ourselves to call by anything other than her full name—was a herpetologist by training, and her office was plastered with lizard photos the way some teenage girls' bedrooms sport wall-to-wall images of Brad Pitt or Justin Bieber. I mean literally wall-to-wall. She especially had a thing for photos where the reptiles stared directly at the camera; to sit in her office was to confront hundreds of yellow lizard eyes, all at once. Including Cathy Horn's. She did look a bit reptilian herself: small dense body, wide flat head, permanent slouch, a kind of squinting blink.

"Is it true," she began, "that you used the word 'narc' in a puppet show recently?"

I thought for a moment. "I might have. As a verb."

"And also the word 'Hitler'?"

"It made sense in context. It was a joke."

"And I hear there have been fart noises."

"The kids love them."

"Listen, Mark," she said. "You do great work here. You're reliable, you're smart. The kids adore you. But we've had complaints from parents this week. Kids repeat things at home, you know. I was thinking of going away to Ecuador for a month next summer. There's a herpetology summit there. It's big. I'm trying to expand into turtles, and Ecuador is turtle heaven. Kismet. There are turtles there the size of my bathtub."

She sighed. "I was thinking of putting you in charge of the summer program. Deputy director would be your new title—which comes with a raise, of course. But I have to say: not like this."

"Oh," I said. "Thanks, Cathy. I'll try to tone it down."

She stared at me with those squinty reptilian eyes. "Do," she said.

When I arrived home, Rachel was there, waiting on the stoop.

"Your address was in our files," she said.

I looked down at her: sitting up straight, spine primly erect, hands around her knees, eyes wide behind her thick glasses. Her presence here seemed somehow both uncanny and inevitable.

"So you're here to check my proof of residence?" I said. "How thorough of you."

"You haven't been back to the library."

"No. I haven't." I sat down next to her. "Aren't you cold, sitting out here?"

"Not really. I'm wearing long underwear. I knew I might be waiting awhile." She sighed. "I got worried. I started to think maybe I freaked you out."

I looked down at my feet. "Well," I said. "Maybe a little."

"Sorry."

"It's okay. Are you mad at me?"

"Mad at you?" She frowned. "No. Of course not."

"You seemed mad that day."

"I wasn't mad," she said. "I was just a little scared."

"Of what?"

"I just—" She shook her head. "It's hard to explain."

"Do you want to try?"

216

"I guess so. I mean, yes. But I don't really know where to start."

"Well, *I* have a question," I said.

"Okay."

"When I touched your arm, there in the bar—did you feel something...weird?"

At this, her face drained of all color.

"Are you okay?" I asked.

She slowly reached out to touch me, extending her arm toward my leg. As her touch approached, I felt it again: that tingly sensation I'd experienced when I'd touched her in the bar. This time it was even more pronounced, perhaps because she was moving so slowly. She let her hand linger about an inch from my knee, and the feeling grew so strong that I found myself staring at the space between her hand and my flesh, looking for some kind of visual explanation: a crackle of electricity? A carbonated fizzing of the air? A thousand hair-thin needles?

Then she made contact. Her hand grasped my knee, and the feeling grew even stronger. It was as if my knee had suddenly fallen asleep, except that it actually felt more *awake*. It was terrifying. It was also erotic. I could feel my body stirring to meet this mysterious sensation. It reminded me of the feeling I'd had in the dream, with the bats. Before I could respond, though, she quickly withdrew her hand. I turned to look at her. Her eyes were dark and serious.

"You mean *that*?" she said.

"Yes. That."

"Well, remember how I told you I knew someone who had died?"

"Uh-huh."

"Well. That feeling? That's *him*."

THOMAS

At first, Rachel loved having an invisible boyfriend. She said it was what she'd always wanted: a togetherness that resembled the best kind of aloneness. Perfect consonance, zero conversation. A slow constant stretch of desire. A thoroughly weightless lover. A penetration by silence.

Nothing separated us. My "body" seeped into hers. We breathed each other. I couldn't speak any words, but it didn't matter: I communicated through a shifting of texture and pressure, through swarm and whisper and tease.

You may have fantasized before about becoming invisible—you've considered the high-dollar items you'd pilfer, keyholes you'd slip into, people you'd tickle or sucker punch, laughing your silent laugh while they swatted helplessly at the charged air around their bodies. You'd be the ultimate knower of secrets. You could insert yourself into any open space, no matter how tight or forbidden, and in this way your entire existence would become a kind of fucking.

As it turned out, I had no interest in stealing. But fucking, on the other hand? The fucking was fucking fantastic. No worries about getting soft or exhausted; I was no longer bound by the body's laws. I entered Rachel in bed, in the shower, through her thin cotton leggings while she cooked dinner. She'd scold me half-heartedly, trying to suppress a smile.

In my previous life, I was never much of a cuddler. I'd spoon the girl for a few minutes like a gentleman, I'd put in my time—but then I'd roll away, staking my own blanketed terrain, trying to ignore the soft stink of her longings.

Now, though, I could touch Rachel everywhere and still not touch her at all. This paradox incited my keenest colonial impulses: every movement created new pockets of emptiness, calling out to be conquered and occupied. The horizon of her body was always receding, even as she submitted herself, over and over and over. It drove me crazy.

All the Hallmark metaphors? Now, physical facts. *You're my world. You complete me. I'm nothing without you.* Whatever was left of me—a breezy sweep, a tingle of loose molecules—only became activated within a few inches of her body. She had to leave me, of course, for hours at a time—to go to work, to purchase necessities—and during these times I'd feel my existence diffusing, growing thinner. I could still move around if I wanted to, but I moved driftingly, like a cloud; my mind grew fuzzy, I lost proprioception, became just a vague woolly consciousness with no sense of space or time. Memories blended unevenly with the present. Time became palpable and viscous, a lumpy substance in which I could slowly flail for hours. Then I'd hear Rachel's key in the lock and I'd snap back into the present; pressing up against her, I'd feel my nameable parts return like phantom limbs. Shoulder, thigh, cock.

She could not make such distinctions. For her there were no shapes, only two categories of space: Thomas and Not Thomas. "Surround me," she'd say at night. "Let me feel you everywhere." We fell asleep like that, her hot breath dissolving into the ghosts of my bones.

My world had been pleasurably reduced in scale. No outside forces to battle, no one to protect or to fail, only this one body, hers: the lush curving topography of it, the smooth shoulder, the seashell whorl of the ear, the inner thigh's musky scoop. And her face! Staring into space, red lips slightly parted, eyes unfocused; or squinting into her computer screen while eating soba noodles in the kitchen at night; or lightly frowning in the middle of a dream—it changed like the surface of deep water, absorbing and reflecting different kinds of light, its ripples both predictable and deeply mysterious. I lived for what lapped to the surface, half revealed itself, receded. She was like the ocean. There was enough here to interest me for another whole lifetime.

If this sounds obsessive—well, it was. It was also an enormous relief. Finally, someone interested me enough that I could forget about myself. There was plenty worth forgetting.

So when I survived my own disappearance, I felt invincible. As long as I didn't leave the sweet cocoon of my lover's house, no one could get me. I hadn't been back to my apartment in over a month; I'd never know whether the letter had ever come for me, the one from the Office telling me how to return. For all I knew, I'd forfeited my chance anyway, by disobeying their instructions. I didn't care: now I had no desire to return. As long as I didn't go back to my old place, I could forget I'd ever died. I could pretend this was how I'd always intended to live; I could inhabit this two-person universe forever.

Truly, at first, it felt as though we'd *won*—and not only in my game of chicken with the Office. We'd won at love, in general. We'd found it, what everyone wants, the apotheosis of what all the love poets have yearned for: the wet dream of John Donne, the wild fantasy of Rumi. Chagall's lovers floating up toward the ceiling and then past it, into some perfect ether.

But that feeling could only last so long. Because in the end, only one of us had achieved this transcendence; the other, for better or worse, still possessed a body.

* * *

Throughout my deterioration, I'd developed an almost erotic relationship to the apartment itself—to its furniture and blankets, its textures and smells. It had become an extension of my body—and then, as my body deteriorated, a replacement for it. To remain there, even on the long lonely days while she worked at the library, was to remain with myself, inside myself, which was to say with *her*.

Then one night, about two weeks after my "disappearance," Rachel didn't come home. At first I worried that there'd been some terrible accident—that she'd been caught in a subway derailment or sideswiped by a truck, that the library had burned down. But as the minutes ticked by I came to feel certain, deep down in my ghost bones, that she was staying away by choice. It hardly mattered why; what mattered was that she could inhabit a reality that did not include me.

Finally, around midnight, I heard her key in the door, watched her tiptoe inside. I swarmed her instantly, followed her into the bedroom, surrounding her like a cloud of gnats.

"I'm *sorry*," she said, flopping down on the bed with all her clothes on. "I just went over to Jimmy's. I had to talk to someone. I was going crazy. I mean, I didn't *tell* him tell him, of course. I made something up."

She raised her hands, put her palms over her eyes. "I

don't know what to do," she whispered, her voice edged with held-back tears. "I feel like I'm dissolving from the outside in. It's like I can't tell the difference between you and me anymore. I can't touch anything without touching you. I keep having these nightmares, and I don't even think they're *mine*. Just this deep, deep blackness, and then a scream."

Your death is a terminal condition; while it is technically incommunicable, certain symptoms of it may be transferred to others. It was true that I'd heard her toss and turn and cry out in the grip of nightmares. But I hadn't seen this as a "symptom"— not even when she awoke hollow-faced, with bruise-like circles under her eyes. It hadn't occurred to me that as I inhaled the warm heat of her body, as I took in her moist breath and sweet sweaty scent, she was breathing me in too—that there was an economy of life force, an equal exchange. And no living human body had been designed to breathe in another's ghost twenty-four hours a day, like a noxious gas. The more I pleasured and surrounded her, the more of her vitality I absorbed, the more I seeped into her: my memories, my darknesses, my regrets.

For the first time since disappearing, I wished I could speak. Words hadn't seemed necessary before, in our contextless world. But now the lack of language was stifling, like a lack of oxygen.

She turned onto her side; I wrapped myself around her, spooning her from behind, nuzzling the nape of her neck, inhaling her scent. She closed her eyes and leaned into me, accepting the embrace—but for the first time since I'd disappeared, I felt something press against my happiness, dull and metallic, like a blade against the jugular; even this was a bubble, easily pierced.

When you're a ghost, I learned, your human lover will eventually long for a human touch. When she thinks you're not looking, she'll close her eyes and wrap her arms around herself, imagining an embrace. Or she'll walk so quickly from one room to another that you slip off her, unable to catch up: "I just need to feel the air on my skin," she'll say. "The *regular* air. The air that doesn't *want* anything from me."

Despite her feelings for you, however genuine and singular, your lover is a person, in a body. She'll tell you it's not lust that makes her yearn for other bodies, that she doesn't want to replace you—but the difference won't matter. All you will feel is the sting of betrayal as she struggles to affirm her membership in a world to which you no longer belong. You'll feel wounded by her inability, or unwillingness, to fully disappear into you, the way you've disappeared into her.

You'll learn, the hard way, that death is not a disease that others can catch from you. Instead, it makes *you* the disease. Once death has happened to you, it never stops happening. The more you resist it, the harder it rides you.

This is how you become a haunt: skittish and terrified, you grasp after something that no longer belongs to you. You grasp after life. Like a vampire, or a cannibal, you attach to the life of another. You inhale, you swallow.

Fighting with your lover is difficult. You cannot speak. You can barely even displace objects; you can't move a pen across paper with enough precision to make recognizable marks. When you're mad you may resort to childish tactics, like hiding in corners or behind furniture, until she has no choice but to walk through her apartment, swiping the air for a tingly trace of you, begging you back.

When you both tire of such games, you'll develop more sophisticated techniques. (You didn't need these before, when you were happy.) You might try a system in which you squeeze her right hand for "yes," her left for "no." You'll be surprised at how quickly this works, the first time you try it. She'll understand immediately; she'll be so relieved she'll start squealing, then burst into tears. You'll think of Helen Keller with her w-a-t-e-r. Understanding will flow over and between your hands like liquid. After that, inebriated by success, you may undertake some doomed experiments with Morse code.

But no matter what techniques you develop, the substance of the fight will remain the same. You have one irreconcilable difference: she exists, among other bodies, and you do not.

You'll fight this fight so many times that, for all your supernatural tricks, you'll become just like any other troubled couple, locked in that familiar rusted-out cycle: wound, sulk, supplicate, scream. Hate sex, love sex, fragile truce. Lather, rinse, repeat.

You'll eventually have to accept that she has the freedom to go where she wants, to see whomever she desires. But wherever she goes, you'll accompany her—to the grocery store, to her job, to the dentist. Wherever she goes, you follow. You've become more than her lover: you've become her double, her shadow, her ghost.

This is where he comes in: the other man.

There *will* be another man, there's no avoiding it. Through him, you'll discover it's not only love that can strengthen your physical presence. Any strong emotion will do. Hatred, for example. Jealousy works just fine. Your possessive rage will whittle you down to a single purpose.

For a while, at least, this will work in your favor. You'll willingly leave your lover for hours at a time now, not even missing her when you're with the Other Man, because you have an interest in him too—a different kind, of course, but just as strong. You'll discover that you can visibly affect the other man without even touching him—just hover next to him, whisper in his ear. Tell him all the sad parts of your story. Exhale the ambient sorrow of the bodiless. Remind him, your tongue full of venom, that he'll die someday too.

He won't be able to hear you. He'll understand anyway. Your monstrous yearning will invade him till he crumples. He won't be able to explain what has happened to him, so he'll start to doubt himself—and then he'll start to doubt everything.

Even better: while you're off bothering the Other Man, your lover will miss you. She'll worry that you have left her for good. This uncertainty will benefit you. Also, the man himself will come to associate his sadness and confusion with your lover. He will search for solace, for physical distraction, wherever it's most handy—perhaps, if you're lucky, with another lover, one who has her own reasons for maintaining and hoarding his attention.

But don't get complacent. He may move away from your lover only to boomerang back with greater force. Nothing is sexier, after all, than a mystery.

I thought I knew this guy, "Mark." For a while I thought of him like that, in quotes, as if he wasn't real. In my mind he was less a person than a type of person—like a "Ted" or a "Bill" or even a "Chad," he was a generic male, an outline: an actor in a commercial, a figure in a cartoon.

A "Mark" is a very particular, recognizable kind of man. Every elite American college is liberally populated with genial Marks, genially greeting each other at the lab or the gym or the frat party with genial fist bumps or slaps on the back. They are genial males whose lives have been prearranged for maximum ease, to give them the illusion that they've earned their success through their bland, genial competence.

Marks usually come from Westchester or the Waspier parts of New Jersey, or sometimes the Midwest; like the cheerful animals in Richard Scarry books, they aspire toward the most useful, legible professions (doctor, lawyer, owner of a business). They work hard but not too hard, date girls who are pretty but not too pretty, speak loudly and confidently but not *too* loudly and confidently. They aren't assholes, Marks. They're likable. If all the men you knew were Marks, you'd probably conclude that the world was a safe place, filled with good people.

When I first learned about him, in one of those meandering conversations early on, it didn't surprise me that Rachel had a Mark in her past; nor did it surprise me that he had remained there. It's understandable: a Mark arrives, presents himself in a lonely young woman's life, invites her to be his girlfriend. This seems like a good opportunity, making a boyfriend of this nonthreateningly handsome young man who resembles the boyfriends she's seen on TV. She enters the relationship the way a little girl picks up Barbie and Ken dolls, lines them up in bed next to each other, waits for something to happen next. In his kind, pragmatic way, the Mark initiates the young woman into romance and sex. Or perhaps she initiates him, bending and flexing him like a smooth plastic doll into the positions she's imagined in advance.

After an appropriate period, the young woman has a choice to make. Is this Mark enough? Does he comfortably fill the hollows carved out by her teenage longings? If not—if her imagination exceeds the contours of her particular Mark's personality—then she'll grow dissatisfied, lonely, namelessly sad. Perhaps she'll stay with her Mark anyway, but more likely she'll begin to search out other men, men with jagged edges and sharp curves.

Perhaps she'll feel herself inexplicably drawn to men bent into intriguing shapes by their own cruelty, or the cruelty of others. Perhaps she'll find a man so inflated by his own imagination that, for a while, he actually seems larger than life. She'll be thrilled and disappointed, thrilled and disappointed all over again—until she finally locates a workable shape or settles for a second Mark, whose smooth predictability now feels like kindness and perhaps, if she's lucky, actually is.

In my life, my first one, I'd never felt threatened by Marks. I was the second kind of man, the dangerous kind, the anti-Mark. I made women feel alive by hinting at the depth and singularity of my pain, bringing them in touch with their own. I never stayed very long—as an anti-Mark, I couldn't—but I never deceived them either.

But now that I'd become a ghost, I recognized this Mark as the threat he was. If anyone could steal my human girlfriend away, it would be someone like him: someone solicitous and calming, someone solid as a tree and smooth as a baby, someone who had never known death. His kindness was clear to the dumbest of beasts. His generic affability, his boring good looks, might in time induce a calm forgetfulness. His touch might erase my own.

You may have read books, or seen movies, about hauntings—the rustling of curtains, the inexplicable flushing of toilets, the flickering of candles, even good old Patrick Swayze slow-dancing to "Unchained Melody." That's kid stuff. Haunting is not confined to the realm of ghosts. It is a state of avoidance and obsession. We haunt because we are haunted. Every haunter is also a hauntee. You could argue that I'd been haunted my whole life: first by the angel, then by Therese, even perhaps by my mother.

Well, I know all this now. Now I see that I'd been thinking of love as something that happened between only two people. I'd been doing the math wrong: love requires three. The two primarily involved and the third, who serves as an obstacle, an inducement, a reason for the two to come together in the first place—and, once they do, as an invisible audience. But no, the geometry is more complex yet: each lover brings a different third into the room—and each third, in turn, might be trying to escape the pull of some nagging presence or absence. Every individual love story takes place within a larger fabric of desire, stretching out infinitely, pulled from every possible direction. When you think about it, it's miraculous that anyone sticks together at all.

Rachel's real life was still happening. It would keep unspooling—a line stretching infinitely, hazily forward; a snake eating the future. Whereas mine was a circle inscribed by her touch, a snake eating itself. I was living on borrowed time, in a borrowed ghostbody. If I left her, she might be sad for a while; if *she* left *me,* I had no reason to exist.

I threw myself between them, tried to push them apart. But of course the rivalry was no rivalry at all. This aimless overgrown frat boy may have had nothing on me in my former life—in my former life I could have fucked *circles* around him—but, unlike me, he existed. He had that advantage. His big dumb hand just cut right through me, as through air: the ultimate emasculation.

Still, he *felt* me as I raged against him. I could tell. It gave me a small thrill: I might not have been able to physically force them apart, but I could make my presence known. I thought of J. Robert Oppenheimer quoting the Bhagavad Gita: "I am become death, destroyer of worlds." I thrummed with sudden drunken clarity: I was back in the game.

I took great satisfaction in watching Rachel suffer. *Yes, squirm and flail, you stupid little girl, in your stupid human body. Just try to pretend it was ever possible to hold yourself together—that death wasn't always licking at the edges of your life, that the worms and maggots weren't already snapping at the sweet scent of your flesh, that time wasn't eating your pussy with its barbed tongue, that the shit and blood passing out of your body, which you flush away without even looking, was not always a reminder that your body never belonged to you; it was always already disintegrating, leaking, provisional, on loan from the kingdom of bone and snail and ash.*

You've enjoyed your flirtation with death; you've enjoyed your round of slumming in this metaphysical ghetto. But you've forgotten something: for me this is no flirtation. This death is the only life I have left. And I will not be abandoned. I can swallow you whole.

MARK

"So let me see if I've got this right," I said. Nearly ninety minutes had passed. The neighborhood had descended into chilly dusk, the streetlights had come on, and we were still sitting on the stoop. "You met him *after* he died?"

"Right."

"But you didn't know he was dead."

"Right."

"And then he started falling apart, and then he disappeared completely."

"Correct. That was—let's see, a little over a month ago."

"And now he's still *here*? Like a ghost?"

"I guess that's the word for it. It feels weird to call him that, though."

"But is he, like, *conscious*? Can he hear us talking right now?"

"Yes. I mean, I assume so. He's not happy, I can tell you that much."

"How do you know?"

"Because when I'm with you, he tries to get in between us. That's what you felt." She swiped her hand through the air in front of her. "Right now I can't feel him. He's probably somewhere nearby, sulking."

"So a *jealous* ghost."

"I guess so."

"Great." I sighed. "Can't you just ask him to leave? Or *make* him leave somehow?"

"And then what? He dies forever?"

"I don't know."

"I just—" She stopped herself, closed her eyes, swallowed. Her voice was small and tight. "I just have this feeling that I can't go on much longer like this. Something bad is going to happen. I don't know what. But I've barely talked to anyone for months. I go through the motions—I go to work, I pay my rent—but I don't have a *life*. I basically dropped all my friends. When I see them, I can't tell them what's really going on with me. I haven't touched another person since he disappeared—until I ran into you." She sighed. "It's like I can't tell now who's the ghost: him or me. I just sort of float through life but I'm totally apart from it, like there's a glass between me and the world."

I wasn't sure how to respond to this. I was wondering whether now would be an appropriate time to touch her comfortingly—I was just about to reach out and wrap my arm around her shoulders—when she took a breath and continued.

"But I don't *want* him to leave—not exactly. I mean, I love him. And I get so guilty. Like, as if it isn't bad enough that he's already *dead*...Like when I was sitting with you at the bar the other night, I just kept thinking, like, what if he sees this happening? What if, you know, you kiss me or something, and he not only has to watch, but he's right there between us and can *feel* everything? Wouldn't that be, like, the saddest thing in the world?"

"For who?" I said. "For him or for you?"

She sighed. "I don't even know the difference anymore."

We sat there for a minute, letting her words settle, the deepening twilight closing around us like a curtain. Though I'd never believed in ghosts before, I somehow found myself accepting her story. Perhaps it was the fact that I'd felt it too, that strange otherworldly tingle. Or perhaps the months of living with Zoe had primed me for encounters with the uncanny.

But mostly, I think, it was the fact that Rachel was sitting next to me, and she had just—finally—let me in, as I'd wanted her to all those years ago. Perhaps, at last, I had something to offer. As I sat there staring into the lamplit street, the words echoing through my mind were not about the dead man or his ghost. *What if, you know, you kiss me or something?*

"By the way," I said, "I did ask my roommate your question. About...communicating with the dead. Or whatever."

She sat up straight. "And?"

"She gave me this." I pulled out my wallet and

extracted the business card with Dr. Moon's name on it. "I don't know anything about it—all she said was this guy is her guru or something."

Rachel squinted down at the card. "Metaphysical acupuncture," she said. "Huh."

"Listen," I said. "It's getting cold. Would you like to come in for a minute?"

She frowned. "I don't know."

"I'll make you some tea," I said. "We can warm up. And then we can decide, together, what to do."

"Deciding together," she said, slowly. "That sounds nice." She looked up at me. "I didn't mean to drag you into any of this," she said. "But now—I don't know. I guess I'm glad I did."

I stood up and extended my hand. So Zoe had been right, at least partially. "Me too," I said. She took my hand and let me pull her to her feet.

Zoe wasn't home, thank God (or, as she would say, thank Goddess): she had just left for a weeklong yoga retreat in the Berkshires. I let Rachel in and made two cups of tea, then came back into the living room.

She looked thoroughly unrelaxed. She still had her jacket on, and she sat up straight and stiff, the way she did at her library desk.

"Let me take your jacket," I said, setting a mug on the coffee table in front of her. "Come on, make yourself at home."

"I'm still cold," she said. Her voice was flat, drained of warmth. She'd retracted into herself again.

I sat down next to her. "Do you want to borrow a sweater or something?"

"No thanks."

"Is it bothering you? I mean, is he ...?"

She closed her eyes briefly. "I'm just starting to feel like maybe this was a mistake. That maybe I should—"

"Look, have a few sips of tea, you'll feel better. Then we can—"

I was silenced by her mouth on mine. She hadn't so much leaned in to kiss me as pitched forward, her face crashing stiffly into my face, and at first I thought she'd hit me. But then she moved her lips, and I realized what was going on. This was the kiss of a terrified woman. She'd wanted to get it over with; as with any kind of leap, it had to be done immediately and recklessly, or not at all.

I reached out and laid my hands, lightly but firmly, on her shoulders; gently, I drew her closer to me. Then I kissed her, a long kiss, slow and soft. At first, she was still too rigid to receive the kiss properly; she allowed me to touch her, but didn't respond. "It's okay," I murmured. "It's okay." Then I kissed her again, and she softened a little bit. The third time, she actually kissed me back, a proper kiss, warm and wet.

This whole time, it—or he?—pulsed between us, stronger than before, a third presence. It seemed to be

pushing us apart, which had the perverse effect of drawing us closer together; the stronger that tingly feeling
grew, the more desperate I felt to clutch Rachel's body
to mine. It occurred to me that, if her story was to
be believed, I was technically initiating something like a
threesome with a dead guy right now (which was something I doubted even Zoe had done). Yet somehow none
of this bothered me as much as it should have. It only
increased my desire. I kissed Rachel hungrily, and she responded with increasing warmth. The tingling presence
hummed and prickled between us.

I stood up, gently pulled her to her feet, kissed her
deeply. Then I led her by the hand into the bedroom and
we fell, together, onto the bed.

As our bodies tangled, slipping into and around each
other—a pale mix of moonlight and streetlight streaming
through the stained-glass window—I recalled the dream
I'd had, with the bats zinging around the room. I had the
same feeling now—that I was seized by some powerful
entropy, and something was on the verge of escaping
my body.

I couldn't tell you exactly what Rachel's body and my
body did together that night. I only remember certain
moments, like a series of still shots from a movie. These
moments felt timeless and memory-like even as they
were happening: her pale breasts above me; the feeling
of her lips against my skin, just below my belly button;
the low moan her body made when I slid my hand into

her underwear. It was all disjointed and urgent, like a fever dream. The whole time, the ghost pulsed between and around us. The longer the night went on, the more it seemed that we were doing something transgressive— not just socially but in some kind of ultimate way, something that defied the laws of nature. I had the feeling of being suspended over an abyss, as though it was possible I wouldn't survive the encounter.

But I did. I don't remember how it ended, but we must have fallen asleep together. In the morning, though, she was gone.

For the next three nights, Rachel came over. Never with any warning. We hadn't even exchanged phone numbers. She'd just show up and ring the doorbell, or I'd come home and she'd be sitting on the stoop. She always left before I woke in the morning.

We didn't talk. We just fucked. Each night the fucking had the same feeling as it had the first night. The fucking was the disaster; it was also the only way out of the disaster. Each night was its own apocalypse. On the third night she sobbed afterward, as if something was being torn out of her. I said nothing, just held her, and she eventually fell asleep.

Meanwhile, I moved through my days as though in a blur, as though sleepwalking. My mind was maybe 30 percent on whatever I was doing, whatever percentage is the absolute bare minimum necessary to get by; the rest of it was taken up by a delirious reel of images from the night before, of fantasies about the night ahead. I made a few stupid mistakes—I got kids' names wrong, I temporarily forgot the word "marmot"—but I think my absence mostly remained unnoticed. If anything, it was probably seen as an improvement. I certainly didn't get called into Cathy Horn's office again. I had the feeling I was living in two separate realms simultaneously: the one I'd always lived in and this other one, this bright darkness where sex mixed with death, where the present moment felt like a memory and the future didn't exist.

This wasn't exactly what I had imagined when I'd fantasized about getting closer to Rachel. But I did feel, in a way, as though I'd gotten what I'd wanted all those years ago: finally I saw what she was seeing, went where she went.

Sometimes, during the days spent away from her, I grew jealous: her ghost lover was with her right now, and I wasn't. It didn't matter that she was betraying him for *me* (or so I liked to believe; in weaker moments I knew I might have been anyone, that only dumb luck had placed me in her path). I imagined him moving invisibly over her body—in the shower, on the bus, while she slept. Our bodies might come together at night, but he possessed her in a way I never could. I didn't *want* to possess her, not like that—but that didn't stop me from resenting this dead man's ability to do so. It only made things worse to realize, in certain moments of clarity, that in a perverse way I owed it all to him: if Rachel hadn't been haunted by him, she'd never have sought me out as the antidote.

When we made love, there were times when I had the uncanny feeling we were doing it *for* him, for the ghostly other—that Rachel reached out for me only to show him

Many times over the next week I walked past the library. I never went in. It wasn't exactly an issue of courage. It was more like—how do I explain it? As if a curtain had been dropped between us. I'd take a step in the library's direction and feel it pressing against me, almost physically: a sense that I shouldn't go in, and that even if I did, talking to Rachel wouldn't make a difference. Whatever had drawn us together over the last few weeks had turned inside out, become its inverse—as if the magnet's polarity had suddenly switched.

This had nothing to do with desire. I still wanted her. But my desire now lived in some abstract ether of memory and imagination; it had become detached from any actual possibility of our bodies ever meeting again.

As it happened, I never heard from Rachel, or talked to her, again. I probably would have run into her in the neighborhood eventually, but I ended up moving out pretty soon after that, into a studio in Sunset Park. I met my current girlfriend at the coffee shop around the corner.

Rachel wasn't the reason I decided to move. It was because, when Zoe got back from her yoga retreat, she announced that she'd decided to sell the place.

I was stunned; somehow I hadn't realized that Zoe owned the building. It turned out that her dad had bought it in the seventies, and had left it to her when he died of throat cancer two years ago. Her mom had died not long afterward (Zoe didn't say how; the deliberate vagueness carried its own information). Hearing her calmly narrate this backstory, I realized how little I'd actually known about Zoe: between the sexual acrobatics and the bacchanalian parties and the baby bats— all the theatrics and distractions—it had never occurred to me to ask about her family. About anything, really. Perhaps she hadn't wanted me to; perhaps the whole wild woman persona was a smoke screen. I knew Zoe

AMY BONNAFFONS

well enough to guess that she'd hate nothing more than being stereotyped as the Damaged Rich Girl.

Still, I was ashamed of myself. I don't think I'd fully realized, until that moment, how far I had strayed from the idea I'd always had of myself: sturdy, sensible, decent. A good listener. A Good Guy. I'd been living with Zoe for six months, fucking her for five—and in a way, I had barely noticed her.

"God, Zoe," I said. "I'm so sorry. I didn't know any of this."

She shrugged. "I never told you." She pulled her hair back, tying it loosely behind her head. "In any case, what I'm saying is, I felt like I had to hang on to this place and live here. Because of the history. But I've gotten into a rut. I can't just keep teaching yoga classes to hipsters and fucking my roommates." She smiled. "No offense."

"None taken." I wasn't surprised at "roommates," plural; I'd never assumed I was the first.

"In fact," she said, "I have to thank you."

"Thank *me*? For what?"

"It had been a while since I'd been with someone so...kind."

"Kind?" This just made me feel more terrible. It was clear to me now how selfishly I'd behaved.

She smiled. "You're not perfect, Markie," she said. "But you try to do the right thing. That's more than a lot of people do. Being around you made me wonder, what *is* the right thing? For me, I mean." She clasped her

254

hands in front of her chest. "And I think the right thing is to move around a bit. Be a nomad for a little while. Study meditation, work on a farm, whatever. I want to figure out something useful to do with my life, but first I just need to remind myself that the world's bigger than this. Than Brooklyn."

"Yeah," I said. "I guess it is."

"Every place has its ghosts, you know?" said Zoe. "But not all of them are *mine*." I sensed that this last sentence was meant more for herself than for me.

She didn't mention Rachel, or ask whether I'd passed along Dr. Moon's business card. It was as though, with that creepy sixth sense of hers, she already knew what had happened—that that story had played itself out, that the cycle was complete. As for me, I was grateful not to talk about it.

Zoe and I never slept together again—at least, we didn't have sex. But the night before I moved out, she crawled into bed with me and we watched a movie on my laptop. She laid her head against my shoulder; I rested a hand lightly on her thigh. That was it, nothing more.

It felt good to have Zoe's warmth against me like that: just the everyday warmth of a human being, seeking comfort. It occurred to me for the first time that if we'd met under different circumstances—what circumstances, I couldn't say—we might have been friends.

RACHEL

Someone told me once that getting over a relationship takes 50 percent of the relationship's length. If you were together a year, it will take six months; five years will take two and a half, et cetera. I don't remember where exactly I heard this, but I remember being surrounded by women, in some tea or brunch type of situation, possibly accompanied by small pastries and/or knitting, and I remember the other women all nodding when the one woman said this. This seemed accurate to them. They had all independently alighted upon this algorithm of the heart.

I remember sitting there blankly, chewing on my scone or whatever, and feeling puzzled and separate. No man had ever taken me very long to recover from, unless you define "recovery" as "falling back with a vengeance on cherished private habits." After my breakups I had gone for long periods without shaving my legs, or I developed new hobbies like crocheting or pickling, or once I actually read Proust, all of it, in the span of a few weeks. But none of this had ever felt that *bad*. In fact, it had often felt like a kind of gleeful abandonment, the freedom to once again be as singular and strange as I wanted to be.

Now I thought again of the breakup algorithm, and wondered how the math might change if the ex-boyfriend in question had been a ghost. How many years might be added on? Would my grief pass in multiples of seven, like dog years? Or had his world taken such a bite out of me that I'd never be whole again?

All I told Mark was that Thomas was gone. I didn't say any more than that. The details wouldn't make sense to him anyway. I left him to infer the rest: that he and I were done too, for the second and final time.

Frankly, I was a bit embarrassed about the whole thing. Picking up my ex-boyfriend for comfort, like a nubby old blanket. Only women who were babies did things like that. I had always prided myself on not being a baby-woman. In fact, I wasn't a baby even when I was an actual baby. My first full sentence, when I was eighteen months old, was "Don't pick me up." I have always been little and cute, my whole life; my whole life, people have wanted to pick me up and cradle me and treat me like an idiot.

But something had happened to me, living with a ghost. The daydream had turned into a nightmare, and the nightmare had turned me into a child. So I had reached out for my sweet ex-boyfriend with the cowboy grandpa smile. I'm not proud of it. But I found myself in his bed, amid something that was not exactly the daydream, more like its toxic inverse; I pictured it as a sickly green light that surrounded us as we clutched at each other. Those four nights taught me something, something I had already known deep down but had not been able to confirm until then: that I still had a body, that this body wanted other bodies, that it could make contact with other bodies even through the noxious green haze of an angry ghost.

I had been living in the daydream for so long that now I just wanted the most basic things: the warmth of human skin, the weight of another person next to me in bed.

Thomas would never leave me. *I* would have to leave *him*. Only I could extinguish the dying embers of the daydream. To claim my own selfish, boring, pointless life as though it were my only treasure—because, in fact, it was.

When I got home from Mark's, the morning after that fourth night, I picked up the card that he had given me, the recommendation from his roommate, Zoe. It had been sitting on my kitchen table, calmly waiting for my attention.

DR. B MOON
METAPHYSICAL ACUPUNCTURE

The name had sounded vaguely familiar before; only now did I remember that Dr. Moon was the name my doppelgänger had spoken in that dream I'd had one of the first nights Thomas slept over: "I believe these belong to Dr. Moon," she'd said, holding out a pair of ears. "If you'd be so kind as to pass them along."

I called Dr. Moon's office and made an appointment. I was told that he happened to have an opening the next day, that usually his schedule was backed up for months.

"You are so lucky," purred the woman over the phone.

"I don't know if that's the word I would use," I said. She just laughed, and told me to be there by two.

On the subway ride to Dr. Moon's office, I speculated about what "metaphysical acupuncture" might be. Probably some kind of mistranslation. (I assumed from the name, and from racist stereotypes about his line of work, that Dr. Moon would be Chinese or Korean. For some reason I also pictured him with a goatee.)

The office was inside a tall, ugly building near Penn Station, with a grimy urine-smelling lobby and a roster of fake-sounding business names: Apex Consolidated Products, North Star LLC, Synergy Works. Dr. Moon's name wasn't listed anywhere. I rechecked the card and confirmed that I had the address right, then took the creaky old elevator up to the eighth floor, knocked on the unmarked door of room 802, and gently pushed it open.

Stepping into this room was like stepping into a different world, a tiny clean oasis. It was painted a crisp, almost blinding white; a spongy moss-green carpet covered the floor. Two Danish modern chairs were placed next to a stand of bamboo. The walls were unadorned, except for a framed photo of a single pine tree. A slender, black-haired receptionist sat reading a book behind a blond-wood reception desk. Nothing was on the desk, not even a phone.

"Rachel?" she said, looking up from her book with a smile.

"That's me."

"Have a seat," she said. "Dr. Moon will be with you soon; he's journeying at the moment."

"Journeying where?"

She laughed lightly, as if I'd made a joke. Then she went back to her book. We sat there, she reading her book, me hovering nervously in the hard chair, for a full thirty minutes.

"Um?" I said, finally.

"Yes?"

"My appointment was for two. It's two thirty."

"Oh." She smiled again. "Well, Dr. Moon doesn't subscribe to the illusion of time."

"Then why did you tell me to come at two?"

"Don't worry," she said. "All is unfolding exactly as it's supposed to."

I spent the next fifteen minutes fuming, debating whether or not to leave. But when Dr. Moon finally emerged, at two forty-five, I sensed right away that he was the kind of person it's pointless to get mad at. He exuded an evenness, a palpable neutrality, as if he existed in a world different from but contiguous to our own. Getting mad at him would be like throwing rocks at a building protected by an invisible fence. They would just bounce right back in your face.

"Hello, Rachel," he said, extending a hand. It turned out he was tall and blond and clean-shaven, handsome and sexless as a Ken doll. The only strange thing about him: his tiny ears, which were perfect and rosy, like soft little conch shells. Or like the ears of a little girl, soldered to a grown man's head. I had the feeling that his generically perfect body was somehow not "real," that it was a costume of some sort. I can't explain exactly what I mean by that; it's just a feeling I had.

I shook Dr. Moon's hand, then followed him into his office. As I walked past the receptionist's desk, I cast a quick glance at the pages of her book. They were completely blank. She looked up and gave a little wave as I passed.

Dr. Moon and I sat in his office, opposite each other, on two sturdy blond-wood chairs. He looked at me while I looked around the room. It seemed mostly normal: the standard cushioned table covered in butcher paper, the standard wooden desk, the standard framed degree. Except that his degree came from the School of Metaphysical Adjustment Science in Arlesdorff, Switzerland.

I turned back to him, registered his perfect face and his tiny ears. He said nothing. He seemed to want me to speak first, but somehow I didn't feel ready. So we just sat there for a few minutes; he blinked his blond eyelashes and emanated a deep Alpine patience.

Finally, I cleared my throat. "So," I said. "I'm here because—well, it's hard to explain."

"I'll do my best to follow," said Dr. Moon.

"I suppose I'm...being haunted?" I sighed. "Well, to be more precise, I'm in a relationship. With a dead guy. And I don't want to be in it anymore."

"I see," said Dr. Moon. "Was he dead at the time of your first meeting?"

"Yes."

"How dead?"

"Not entirely."

"So on a scale of one to ten?"

"Maybe a three to begin with? And now an eight or nine."

"I see. And the two of you have had sexual intercourse in this state?"

"Many times."

I told him the whole story, beginning at the very beginning: the bus stop and the daydream. Dr. Moon just listened with a perfectly neutral expression. He occasionally nodded, as if confirming an expectation.

When I'd finished, he said, "Is he...with us, at the moment?"

I nodded.

"May I feel your pulse?"

"Okay."

He wrapped two perfect fingers around my wrist, and closed his eyes, and furrowed his brow in a look of deep concentration. I could feel Thomas hovering around me, not touching me exactly but nearby. I could tell that he was nervous, more nervous than angry. I was certain Dr. Moon could feel him too—but he didn't say so. He just felt my pulse, concentrating on it as though it contained the entire story, the history of my body and its longings and their consequences.

Finally he opened his eyes, gave another slight nod, and said, "I know exactly what is going on."

"You do?"

"Yes."

"Can you help?"

"I can," he said. "Here's the problem. You are incredibly porous. Before this happened, you had exactly one hole in your aura. Think of it as an Achilles' heel. That hole is where this man entered."

"Okay…"

"Over the length of your relationship, he has eroded your aura to the point where it almost doesn't exist. It's no wonder you are suffering. You are less like an adult person than like a premature baby. You have no defenses. We need to get you into an incubator. Metaphorically speaking."

"Okay." It made a weird sort of sense.

"So here's what I'm going to do. I'm going to seal up your aura. And meanwhile I'm going to work with your boyfriend."

"Work with him?"

He nodded, curtly.

"How?"

"I am going to help him reverse his regrets."

"His what?"

"It's all a bit complicated. It's probably better if I don't explain." He gestured toward the cushioned table.

I looked from him to the table. I decided that I trusted him, though I wasn't sure why. Plus, I had no other options at this point. I walked over and lay down on the butcher paper.

Dr. Moon put a few small needles into my fingers and toes and temples. Then he switched on some ambient reed-flute music and left.

I lay there for a long time—how long exactly, I couldn't say. I may have fallen asleep; I'm not sure. In any case, I entered a sleeplike state of relaxation, a state of consciousness that was gray and calm and absolute. It was as if I'd been sealed inside a bullet. I couldn't feel Thomas at all. I assumed he had left the room with Dr. Moon.

Slowly and gradually, a bright pain spread across the surface of my body, like a sunburn. It was a kind of pleasurable pain, like when you finally let pee out after

AMY BONNAFFONS

holding it for a long time, or like pressing the edge of
your nail into the center of an itchy bug bite. It hurt, but
it was a relief. I wondered if this was the feeling of my
body sealing itself up.

Time passed—how much, I'm not sure. The pain
sharpened, then subsided. Finally, through a blank haze,
a sound came: Dr. Moon turning the doorknob. He
walked over to the table and began removing the needles
from my body, one by one.

"How do you feel?" he asked.

"I'm not sure," I said. "Good, I think."

He removed the last needle. "Do you think you can
sit up?"

Slowly I raised myself to a sitting position. I felt...not
dizzy exactly, but dazed, as though I'd just emerged from
a drugged sleep.

"Where's Thomas?" I asked.

"He's gone," said Dr. Moon.

I opened my mouth to ask where, but then thought
better of it. I probably wouldn't understand, and I didn't
really want to know. I felt a certain deep numbness that
I needed to preserve; this numbness felt necessary for
my survival.

Dr. Moon helped me off the table. "Get lots of sleep
in the next few weeks, and drink lots of fluids," he said.
"You may need to come back and see me again. If so, just
give my assistant a call. You have our number."

"Thank you," I said.

And just like that, it was over. I left Dr. Moon's office and rode the subway home accompanied only by the strangers on the train and the noises of the city, surrounded on all sides by the normal air of the regular world. My ghost was gone. I was free.

In the months that followed I didn't cry, not once. I couldn't. Instead I carried a small knot between my stomach and chest that, I understood, could not be undone—like that story about the woman with a green ribbon around her neck, and her head falls off when her husband unties it. I didn't know what would happen if I cried, but I knew it would result in just as disastrous an undoing. This knot seemed like a small price to pay for what I'd been through. I had given myself to a dead man; I would have to take life back on its own terms.

To keep myself occupied, I started walking. I walked to the library in the morning instead of taking the bus. When I got off work, I kept walking. I walked all over Brooklyn. Sometimes I even walked to Manhattan or Queens, pulling my coat around me as I crossed the windy bridges, half-heartedly hoping that no muggers lurked, waiting in the shadows, but not really caring much either way. I didn't care much about anything. I barely had a thought.

One day, on one of my walks, I found myself in Samira's neighborhood. I hadn't seen her in months—not since the day I'd run away from her in Brooklyn Provisions. Without giving myself time to second-guess the decision, I walked up to her door and pressed the buzzer.

"Hello?" came her voice through the crackly intercom.

"It's me," I said. "Rachel."

There was a brief pause—I imagined her tilting her head to the side, thinking, *Rachel who?*—and then the buzzer buzzed me in.

When I got to the top of the stairs, Samira was already standing there, in the open doorway of her apartment, practically vibrating with agitation.

Her hair was longer now—not quite its pre-fire length, but almost to her shoulders. "Bitch, where have you *been?*" she cried. Then she embraced me.

I tried to hug her back. I seemed to have forgotten how. Mechanically, I raised my arms and placed them around her shoulders. I realized she was the first person I'd touched since Thomas left. (I'd texted with Jimmy, minimally, but hadn't yet seen him in person—our relationship had been strained since he'd entered the throes of throupledom, since I'd gotten involved with Thomas. He seemed to think I disapproved of his relationship, which I did, but of course that was the least important part of the story; desperate for an excuse, I'd let him believe what he wanted.)

Samira was just so...*warm*. It was almost uncomfortable, her warmth—like looking directly at the sun. Too intense for my current equipment. But I breathed through the hug, tried to receive it. *You are less like an adult person than like a premature baby. You have no defenses.* I'd have to teach myself how to be an adult person again. To respond to normal human decibels of affection, without flinching.

Finally Samira pulled away, held me at arm's length. "What *happened*?" she said.

"A lot happened," I said. "I'm not even sure how to describe it."

"Flor said that Jimmy said that you were dating some super fucked-up guy."

"That's true," I said.

"I got mad at you for disappearing," she said. "Then I got worried about you. Then I just got sad."

"I know. But it had nothing to do with you." I shifted from one leg to the other, as though I had to pee. Then I realized I *did* have to pee. "I'm sorry. Can I come in?"

"Of course."

I hadn't been in her apartment since the night of the fire. There was a blackened spot above the stove that hadn't been there before, and the floorboards in the kitchen were warped. "They haven't fixed this yet?" I asked, incredulous. "What was that, a year ago?"

She shrugged. "Nah. Like, four months? It was my birthday, remember? In August."

It felt like forever ago, a whole lifetime ago. "Still, though," I said. "Your landlord sucks. This is really shitty-looking."

272

She grinned. "I know. Secretly, I kind of like it, though. Like, what if everything that happened in life left an obvious mark? I mean, everything *important*. Like, when you're a kid, your parents mark your height on the wall. You can look back and be like, oh shit, I've grown *this much* this year. When you're older, it's harder. You can't tell when you're making progress. And everyone tries to *hide* what's happened to them. It's confusing. But when you think about it, isn't all experience just *experience*? Shouldn't we treat it all the same?" She fondly patted the black spot on the wall. "This spot says, something happened on my birthday this year." She shrugged. "I know it's silly."

"No," I said. "It's not. I think I know exactly what you mean." I realized, in that moment, how much I had missed her. "I've really missed you," I said.

"I missed you too." She reached out and squeezed my shoulder, then glanced down at her phone on the table, which had just glowed and begun to vibrate. "Oh shit," she said. "I'm late! I forgot Flor's thing was tonight. Her Christmas slash Hanukkah party. Are you going?"

"I wasn't invited."

"Yes you were!"

"I don't think so."

"It was an Evite."

"Oh. I never open those. But still, I don't think I got it."

"It doesn't matter. Come on, why don't we go together? Flor will be *so* happy to see you."

"I don't know. She's probably mad at me for being distant. I mean, I completely forgot her birthday. She's not as forgiving as you."

"Who cares?" said Samira, pulling on a scarf. "She'll forgive you eventually. She's your *friend*."

I sighed. "I guess you're right."

"Come on," she said. "We can talk about it on the train."

And so I reluctantly, yet gratefully, submitted. I took Samira's arm as we walked to the subway, allowed her to shepherd me back into my own life.

Over the next few months, through the bitter cold of winter and the aching thaw of spring, I continued my walks. Over time, they started to feel different—less like I was fighting through something and more like I was heading somewhere, though where that was I couldn't know.

I started, slowly, to spend more time with other people. Even the friends who were skeptical and wounded at first, like Flor, began to show some sympathy when I apologized and told them some version of what I'd been through—about this handsome fucked-up man I'd fallen in love with, who had consumed my life and then suddenly "gone." Slowly, I started getting invited to things again. I said yes to everything.

Conveniently, around daylight savings time, Jimmy's throuple finally dissolved, once and for all—and so again we were single, together. Together we went to costume parties and barbecues and brunches. We attended concerts and poetry readings and bizarre performance art events. Sometimes we even joined the gatherings of strangers; we'd hear some clamor from an upstairs apartment, and we'd buzz to invite ourselves in, and nobody ever questioned our right to be there. We drank anything that anyone put into our hands.

And I slept with anyone who asked. Numbly, uncomplainingly, I took man after man into my bed. Sometimes the sex was good, and sometimes it was awkward. Sometimes I came and sometimes I didn't. Sometimes they left in the middle of the night and sometimes they stuck around in the morning, wanting to cuddle or buy me pancakes.

I didn't care. It was something to do. In some way I couldn't quite explain, I *had* to do it. I felt as though I was finally getting somewhere. Every time someone touched me, every time I felt the friction of another person's skin against mine, I seemed to move closer to something, though I couldn't quite have said what, or why.

Still, often after the latest one-night lover had left, I felt crippled by waves of sadness. I felt as though my heart was a rock that had been thrown to the bottom of the ocean. The more alive I felt, the more I hurt. Sometimes the hurt was literal; sometimes I felt the pleasurable ache I'd had there in Dr. Moon's office, as if my skin was on fire. I could just barely remember how Thomas's touch, or nontouch, had felt. With every new lover I forgot a little bit more. Still, I never cried; the knot in my chest remained.

I never got in touch with Mark to apologize or explain. Perhaps this was cruel, and perhaps this was kind. I didn't know; I still don't. All I knew was that I needed the men I slept with now to be strangers.

Then, at a party one warm night in May, I shared a beer with a guy, and he insisted on walking me home. Some Josh or Jeremy. Josh.

This Josh was earnest and eager to prove his New Man credentials through a thorough, industrious demonstration of oral sex; he dotted his i's and crossed his t's and soon I ascended the slope of a medium-sized orgasm, predictably shaped as a sine wave.

And that's when the strange thing happened. While Josh kept working away down there, a white light appeared behind my eyelids. It got bigger and bigger until it took up the whole darkness, like some kind of eclipse.

Was I dying? Was this the white light people talked about? It did not feel spiritual. It felt terrifying and hostile, like a punch in the eye sockets. Meanwhile, the knot in my chest grew larger and tighter, pushing upward, right up into my throat.

I tried to open my eyes, but they seemed to be stuck shut. I gave a little moan of alarm, which Josh of course took as encouragement. He moved faster and harder, and the light got whiter and more blinding and sort of *vibrated,* and I cried out in fear.

When I finally opened my eyes, Josh was sitting there grinning proudly, as if he'd won the National Sine Wave Graphing Bee of America. I opened my mouth to speak, but instead of speaking, I started to sob.

And sob and sob and sob. Like nothing you have seen or heard of. It was as if all the tears I hadn't cried were suddenly released, all at once. My tears flooded and soaked the whole bed. I tried to stop the flow with my fingers, but that just made the pressure build up, and when I removed them, water flew out at a right angle. It was like *The Exorcist*. Alarmed, unsure whether this spoke well or poorly of his skills as a lover, Josh grabbed me a towel. I soaked through that too, in about one second.

The strange thing was, I didn't feel sad. I didn't feel *anything*. Except surprise, and maybe annoyance at the way Josh kept hovering around me with towels and saying, "Are you okay? Was it something I did?"

"Can you just *go*?" I heaved. Finally he got the hint and pulled on his tighty-whities and fled into the dry Brooklyn night.

Water was still pouring out of me, at an unbelievable rate. I soaked through all of my sheets, four towels, and a spare comforter before the tide finally slowed to a trickle. After changing my sheets I managed to sleep, but I woke the next morning on dampened pillows, still crying. I called in sick to work, and the tears continued all through the next day and the next.

On the third day, unsure what else to do, I dragged myself to the neighborhood clinic and saw a kind Estonian doctor, who pronounced me "fertile as a fiddle." I was glad he got the expression wrong. It made me stop crying for a second. He told me to drink lots of fluids, and referred me to a psychiatrist.

I told the psychiatrist that I had recently been through a difficult breakup, but she did not consider this a sufficient explanation for my strange ailment. She seemed convinced that the breakup had triggered a reaction from some other repressed trauma, some hideous disfiguring incident from my childhood. But I remembered my childhood perfectly, and it was all just fine, a bit boring, even. I had no lecherous uncles or violin teachers, and I never even had the chance to meet a perverted priest since we were not Catholics but Unitarians, who always hang out in big cock-blocking groups. Nevertheless, she prescribed me some antidepressants.

"I don't feel depressed, though," I said. "I actually feel better than I have in a while. Except for the tears."

"You're probably just repressing it," she said. "Your depression."

"Oh."

"By the way, be careful with this medication. One of the possible side effects is suicidal ideation."

"It is?"

"Only for some people."

"Oh."

"So if that happens, call me."

"What if I kill myself first?"

She gave me a look that said This Is No Joking Matter, but I hadn't been joking. I took the prescription home and used it as a bookmark.

Finally I did what I should have done in the first place and called Dr. Moon's office. Once again, he had a "miraculously rare" opening, and was able to see me the next day.

"So," I told Dr. Moon, sitting once again in his tiny bright office. I pointed at my face where I could feel watery rivulets carving paths down the slopes of my cheeks. "This is happening."

Dr. Moon nodded. "For how long?"

"About a week." I told him everything that had happened since I'd last seen him, including the orgasm and the blinding white light. He just nodded again. When I'd finished, he felt my pulse and asked me to lie down on the table. He put needles all over my body, in different places from the time before. I lay there for half an hour. The tears kept coming, blurring the ceiling's rectangular panels into squiggly blobs. My ears filled with warm salty water.

But when Dr. Moon came back and removed the first needle, the flow instantly stopped. As he pulled out the rest of them, one by one, I touched my face all over, sweeping away the preexisting wetness. No new wetness came to replace it. I felt calm, like a landscape after rain.

I sat up slowly, still patting my newly dry face all over to see if I could trust it. "I don't want to speak too soon," I said, "but I think you stopped it."

He shook his head. "I'm not *stopping* your tears. I'm *redirecting* them."

"What, like irrigation?"

He thought for a second. "Yes. Exactly. The human body has an exquisite natural system of irrigation, but sometimes these blocks occur. Some parts of your body become overwatered, others too dry. So all that water builds up somewhere, and no one can use it."

I thought of a tiny family living inside me somewhere, unable to drink or wash their dishes, their faucets dry and dusty.

"In this case," he said, "it was partly due to a natural blockage—a blockage you've always had—and partly due to some side effects of my last treatment."

"Side effects?"

"Last time, I sealed up your aura. It was necessary for your protection. But I sealed it up *too* well. Nothing could get out. Your tears were trapped, which created this eventual buildup and pressured release. Today I've restored the natural flow. Thankfully, your aura is in much better shape than it was a few months ago. I'm gratified to see how much you've healed."

"I don't *feel* healed," I said, surprised at my petulant tone.

Dr. Moon frowned thoughtfully. "Well," he said, "it's a nonlinear process. But I'm not sure you're aware of how much danger you were in when you came in last time."

"What do you mean?"

"You were on the brink of turning inside out. Becoming your own inverse."

"What?"

He shook his head tightly. "I don't think I can explain in layman's terms," he said. "But there was a danger that...well, that some version of what happened to your boyfriend would happen to you too."

"That I'd die?"

He looked thoughtful. "In a sense."

I decided to let it go. There was something else I'd been wanting to ask, though I was afraid. "My ex-boyfriend," I said. "Thomas. What did you—I mean, where did he *go*?"

Dr. Moon cocked his head to the side, thinking. I suppose he was trying to figure out how to put it into words. "Are you familiar with the concept of guardian angels?" he asked.

"Yes."

"Well, they don't exist. But there is another kind of...angel, I suppose...assigned to each of us, somewhat randomly. Though personally, I don't like the term 'angel.' It's misleading. It makes people envision a certain shape or archetype that is just one of many forms this kind of being may take. But in any case, that term is probably the most understandable to people in your culture. So let's call it an angel. I helped Thomas find his angel. Go back to his angel. They had some unfinished business. They were waiting for him."

"Who was? The angel?"

"Among others."

"So he's...in heaven?"

"In a sense."

"What I'm asking is—he's okay?"

"Yes, he's okay. You might even say that he's found peace. The particular version of peace available to him." He furrowed his brow slightly. "Though it may no longer make sense to use the word 'he.'"

"So he's not...mad at me?"

Dr. Moon smiled. I realized this was the first time I'd ever seen this. "No," he said. "Certainly not. You have to realize—he was unwell. And now, whatever else we might say about him...he's not unwell anymore. We might even speculate that in some form, he's...grateful to you. Or something like it."

"Well," I said. "That's a relief." So Thomas was somewhere else, someplace where his existence made more sense. He was no longer a hungry lonely ghost roaming the streets. More importantly, or more selfishly: he would not come back seeking closure or revenge. I could finally let him go.

I let out a long sigh. "These angels," I said. "Do I have one too?"

"Yes. Everyone does."

"Will I ever see Thomas again?"

He paused, considered this for a long time, then said, "In a sense."

I had the feeling I wouldn't get more out of Dr. Moon

than this. But somehow, it was enough. "I have one more question," I said.

"Yes?"

"You said, before, that aside from the side effects of your treatment, I had a natural blockage in my body."

"Right."

"Am I cured?"

"It's not a disease," he said. "It's just how you are."

"So some part of me was not . . . getting enough water?"

"Correct. Some part of you had *always* been starved for moisture."

"But you irrigated me?"

"For the time being."

"What do I do now?"

"Nothing. Everything will unfold exactly as it's supposed to." That phrase again. He held open the door for me. Our session was over. I picked up my bag, smoothed down my hair, and stood up.

"Drink plenty of fluids," he said as I walked out the door.

The phrase had practically lost all meaning by then. But it sounded different, coming from Dr. Moon. Coming from him, the words seemed to describe much more than drinking water. I repeated it in my mind, all the way home. *Drink plenty of fluids.* By the time I got home I didn't know what it meant anymore. It seemed like the most profound and inscrutable directive I'd ever heard.

Back in my apartment, the first thing I did, of course, was pour myself a tall glass of water. I drank it in one gulp, standing up. Then I poured another glass and sat on the couch for a while, sipping steadily, continuing to hydrate.

My body felt light and alert, better than it had in recent memory. Still, something felt wrong, and I was having trouble putting my finger on what. Then it occurred to me: everything was so *quiet*. The air felt deathly still; it was as if my apartment had died. I hadn't realized it, but over the past week the tears had provided a sort of soundtrack to my life, a background murmur, like the "Zen fountain" water feature in my parents' overlandscaped backyard. The new tear-free silence felt both obvious and frightening, like a naked mannequin, or the truth.

I walked through all three of my apartment's small rooms, humming to myself and rustling the edges of magazines to try and disperse this silence, but each time it just regrouped and stood its ground. Its occupation was complete and hostile. This silence did not want to penetrate me; it wanted to obliterate me. In self-defense

I stood in the middle of my living room and spoke my own name three times. My objects just stared back at me, pleading and mute.

This silence, I knew, was the strangled nonvoice of a certain kind of emptiness. Not the kind of emptiness I'd known with Thomas—a sexy emptiness, an emptiness that had fucked me and fought with me and filled me up. This emptiness was just a big old nothing, a simple absence of other living things, a completely dead deadness. I supposed it had been there long before I met Thomas, but it had never really bothered me before. Now it was frank, blinding, unavoidable.

I suddenly felt exhausted. I stretched myself out on the couch, pulled the threadbare afghan over my legs, and fell asleep.

I dreamed I was holding my heart in my hand. It bulged wetly, redly, out of my palm. It was still beating, though it wasn't connected to anything. This was an ability I had gained: the ability to remove my own heart at will, to look at it for a while and then put it back.

I brought the heart up to my face, squinched one eye shut, and peered down into the left ventricle.

At the other end of the wet red tube was a plushly furnished room in the style of middle-upper-class America circa 1920. A large brass Victrola piped tinny music into the room. Somber, sepia-toned family portraits hung on the walls. The parents sat on an overstuffed pink velvet sofa, one of the children in a large blue armchair, the other perched atop the ottoman at the armchair's feet. They all sat still, in attentive postures, listening to the music.

All of them were blindfolded and gagged.

I lowered the heart and watched it. It pounded faster and faster in my hand, in fear of what it now knew about itself.

Some part of you had always *been starved for moisture.* I knew exactly who these blindfolded people were: they were the family I had pictured earlier, living in my heart, suffering mutely through its seemingly endless drought. I pictured their dry dusty faucets, the hollow clink of their empty water glasses. I understood that I had not exactly been responsible for the drought itself—*It's just how you are*—but that I *was* responsible for their silence: I myself had blindfolded and gagged them, because I had known that they were suffering, and I hadn't wanted to hear them complain.

Steeling myself, inhaling deeply, I raised the heart to my eye again and looked inside. Then, somehow, aided by the miraculous physics of dreams, I made myself very very small, and I entered my own heart: sliding down the mucus-slick muscular tube, landing on the carpeted living room floor with an ungraceful *thunk.*

The family seemed aware of my arrival, in the way that they sat up a bit straighter, in the sudden perk of their posture and expressions. But they emitted no sound, attempted no struggle. I knelt down in front of them. One by one, I removed their blindfolds and gags: the two parents on the sofa, the girl in the armchair, the boy on the ottoman.

None of them spoke, even when liberated from restraint; each just looked at me frankly, with both severity and kindness. All of their eyes were exactly the same: their eyes were mine.

I stood up and addressed them. "There's water for you now," I said. "At least, there should be."

They smiled and nodded, but still they said nothing.

"Isn't there anything you want to say?" I pursued.

They cocked their heads to the side, frowned. One by one, they shook their heads. But then the littlest one—the boy—got up, walked across the room to the Victrola, paused to give me a meaningful look, and then switched off the music.

I had forgotten it was on. I'd only been aware of its tinny, tinkling melody in the subconscious way that one registers any ambient noise: the hum of a furnace, the trilling of crickets or birds. This music seeping out from the tiny Victrola had been the little-noticed, ever-present soundtrack of my heart—and now, the little boy had turned it off. The silence was deafening.

He looked up at me with an air of gentle challenge. Then he spoke. "What are you going to do now?" he said.

I stared back at him, speechless. I had no idea what I was going to do. I had never felt so blank, so void of ideas. Yet a sentence arrived fully formed on my tongue: "I'm going to get a new bed," I announced.

The boy gave a slow nod of approval. "And where will you find this new bed?" he asked.

I thought for a second. "In reality," I said.

Again, he nodded. "Reality," he said, "has the most comfortable beds." Then he turned to his family, who had been watching our conversation attentively, and addressed them. "Why don't we play a game of checkers or tiddlywinks?" he said.

They nodded and smiled.

I understood that my job here was done, that our conversation was over, that the family in my heart needed no further services from me at this time. Hazily, slowly, I awoke; I left the little room inside my heart, I left the little family, I opened my eyes onto my own living room, which looked just the same as before. But the question still rang in my ears. *What are you going to do now?*

I ordered a new mattress off the Internet. It arrived at my apartment in an impossibly small-looking box; when I cut open the box, the mattress sprang forth from within, like Athena from the head of Zeus: a new idea, fully formed. The mattress was large, a queen, and covered in the whitest cloth I had ever seen. Its whiteness was blinding, astonishing; it filled up my shabby, dimly lit bedroom like a soft rectangle of light. It fit perfectly, snugly, into the new wooden bed frame I'd bought from Ikea. Staring at this mattress, I knew that I had fulfilled the directive from my dream: to purchase a bed that was entirely new, that had been manufactured in reality. It was clear, even just by looking at it, that this mattress had been conceived and assembled in a spirit of American ingenuity, with its brilliantly bleached cotton fibers and its newfangled memory foam and its adherence to international standards of fair trade and environmentally friendly manufacturing. This mattress had never known the touch of bodily fluids or disappointment or death. Nothing bad or strange had ever occurred atop its surface.

It's a little on the nose, I thought, addressing the boy

from my dream. *As a metaphor, I mean.* But I knew, without having to wait for an answer, what he would say in response: that at some point the distinction between metaphor and reality grew specious, that the saggy old mattress I'd dragged down to the curb that morning was simultaneously an idea and an actual object and a stale sponge of dead dreams, that its relationship to the ghost who had slept on it was more than associative, more than metaphorical or metonymic. If I had learned anything over the course of the past year, it was that there was even less distinction than I'd thought between inside and out, between one body and the next, between solid and liquid and gas and memory.

Which was why it made sense, now, for me to try and work from the outside in—to begin not with my mind but with the furniture. I sat down on the new mattress, felt its gentle yet firm resistance. I swept a hand across its surface.

I was done sleeping with random men. I would sleep by myself until I could find one worthy of this mattress's newness, its innocence, its utter freshness as an object. By which I meant a man who lived in reality: not the reality of memories and ghosts and dreams, but the consensual reality of ordinary life, the reality to which I had been born and yet had never fully claimed. The reality from which I had attempted to depart, and in which now I must endeavor to stay.

ACKNOWLEDGMENTS

A book begins its life as a kind of daydream. I'm grateful to the many people who helped me guide this one into tangible form, into shared reality.

Thank you first of all to my agent, Henry Dunow, who took a chance on this book when only half of it existed; who read several full drafts and spent hours on the phone with me, discussing its characters and cosmology; who advocated passionately for my work when my own enthusiasm was in question; and whose humor, heart, and straight talk were always just the medicine I needed to keep going.

Jean Garnett, my incredibly smart editor, immediately comprehended this book in its totality: its heart, its bones, its nervous system. Her expert edits and reflections gave it strength and vitality.

I am grateful to Lee Boudreaux and Reagan Arthur for bringing *The Regrets* to Little, Brown, where I've been treated with such kindness. My talented team there includes Elora Weil, Carina Guiterman, Katharine Myers, Ira Boudah, and Karen Landry. Julianna Lee is responsible for the killer cover design, and Mio Im for the illustration.

I had the privilege to work on this book at several

amazing residencies, some of which supplied me with generous fellowships. Thank you to the Centre d'Art i Natura, Writers Omi at Ledig House, Dorland Mountain Arts Colony, the MacDowell Colony, Brush Creek Foundation for the Arts, the Virginia Center for the Creative Arts, the Writers' Colony at Dairy Hollow, and Caldera Arts. Thank you also to the Creative Writing Program at the University of Georgia.

Endless gratitude to the brilliant friends and mentors who read earlier versions of this book and provided crucial feedback: David Busis (who read several drafts), Axel Wilhite, Boris Fishman, Reginald McKnight, Helen Rubinstein, and Peter Cook. Other writerly comrades helped with sections of the novel: Shamala Gallagher, Kseniya Melnik, Mariah Kess Robbins, Sativa January, Ellen Reid, Amanda Altman, Colin Shepherd, Anna North, Vauhini Vara, Anna Kerrigan, Sam Forman, and Stephen O'Connor.

This book took a long time to write. Deep gratitude to the many people who've sustained me over the course of the work, nourishing me with love in its many forms: my incredible parents; my fantastic sister; the rest of my family, living and passed; the wonderful man with whom I share a house and a life; my wise and intrepid dream tenders; and my dear ones locally in Georgia and scattered around the world, for whom "friend" feels like too weak a word (you are my family too). I'm so glad I get to be on this side of the veil with you all.

ABOUT THE AUTHOR

Amy Bonnaffons is the author of the story collection *The Wrong Heaven* (Little, Brown, 2018). She was born in New York City and now lives in Athens, Georgia. *The Regrets* is her first novel.